Traveler

Join the fun by adding your comments on this book at:

travelerbike.blogspot.com

Thank you.

Other books by David Cheever

Daytrips Hawaii
Daytrips San Francisco
Pohaku
Belt Collins
A Close Call
Historic Corridors
Envision

Traveler

David Cheever

authorHOUSE®

AuthorHouse™
1663 Liberty Drive
Bloomington, IN 47403
www.authorhouse.com
Phone: 1-800-839-8640

Published by AuthorHouse 4/9/2013

ISBN: 978-1-4817-1951-3 (sc)
ISBN: 978-1-4817-1952-0 (e)

Library of Congress Control Number: 2013903206

Traveler's Travels

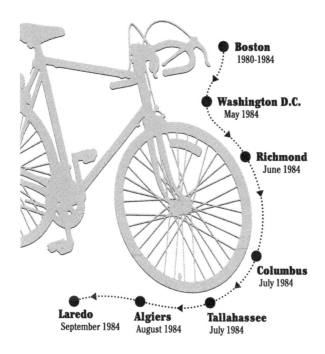

Boston
1980-1984

Washington D.C.
May 1984

Richmond
June 1984

Columbus
July 1984

Laredo
September 1984

Algiers
August 1984

Tallahassee
July 1984

Table of Contents

Prologue ....*ix*

Chapter 1 **Boston** 1980 - 1984 .... *1*
Finally, medical school for Matt

Chapter 2 **Washington, D.C.** May 1984 25
Bike helps Man meet Woman

Chapter 3 **Virginia** May 1984 55
Escape from home on the bike

Chapter 4 **Richmond** June 1984 69
So much to learn

Chapter 5 **Columbus** July 1984 93
A horrible incident

Chapter 6 **Tallahassee** July 1984 121
Big, bigger, biggest

Chapter 7 **Algiers** August 1984 141
Very French

Chapter 8 **Boulder** 1975 159
So this is what happened

Chapter 9 **Laredo** September 1984.................187
      The bad people appear

Chapter 10 **The Wedding**....................................215

Acknowledgements...227

Prologue

In 2012 I was working in a small non-profit used bike store called Wiki Bikes. One day a man rolled in two bikes, one in each hand. "I'd like to donate these. Do you want them?" In his left hand was a non-descript kid's bike and in his right was a dusty old road bike.

We were very busy. I looked quickly and saw the road bike was an old Schwinn Traveler model, a classic from the 80s. "I hate to give up my Schwinn because it got me to medical school and my residency for seven years. I trusted it the whole time and it never let me down. But here."

I said thank you and he was gone.

When I thought about it later in the day, when things calmed down, here was a bike – the doctor's Schwinn Traveler – with a history; a valuable piece of equipment. A story, if you will. So the old Traveler was the inspiration for this novel.

This book starts out with a character named Matt, who is admitted to medical school in Boston. It's all fiction after that. Hope you like it.

Boston 1980 - 1984

Finally, medical school for Matt

All afternoon she had been listless. It was partly because of what had come in the mail earlier and partly because she didn't like being home from work with a migraine. After her headache got better she cleaned a kitchen cupboard and dusted books on one of the high shelves. But just as soon as Janell heard the door knob turn, she grabbed the big envelope on the kitchen counter and rushed to greet him. The smile on her face was restrained. He was hardly in the door when she handed him the envelope.

"Do you think? It's addressed to you and it says Tufts University School of Medicine Admissions and it feels thick. I can't stand it. Hurry and open it."

Matthew started to smile now, but her look remained mildly anxious. He gave her a kiss on the cheek and said, "Could I at least put down my backpack and hang up my coat?" The envelope opened easily and he pulled out most of the contents. On top was a letter dated April 3, 1980 that said, "Congratulations Matthew Hudson. You have been selected to attend Tufts Medical School class of 1984." Without reading further he handed her the letter and headed for his desk.

1

"Oh Matt. This is so exciting. This is your dream. Medical school." She didn't want to recall the last two years when Matt had applied to six different medical schools with the same results. Disappointment after disappointment. She was convinced it had nothing to do with his academic success and everything to do with that terrible incident Matt suffered through in Boulder as an undergraduate. Time and again Janell marveled at him for not caving in to painful rejections and instead, those seemed to make him even more determined.

"The world famous, revered Tufts Medical School. I couldn't be happier for you. When the mail came today, I wasn't sure what was inside that envelope, but since it was thick I thought maybe, just maybe. I couldn't stand it. I almost called you at the lab," she said. In his mind, his innovative work in biochemistry at the MIT lab could have been in part responsible for admission to Tufts.

"I am excited too. At 31, I wasn't sure if my age would work against me. But you are almost more excited than I am. I can tell by the way you're bouncing around the apartment," Matt said.

"Yes. I admit it. I am very excited for you. I confess that since the mail came today, I have worked out a plan for this evening." And she went over to his desk and from behind gave him a lengthy hug. "I put together Plan A to celebrate. I didn't want a Plan B so nothing would be jinxed." She turned him around, put him in his desk chair, then sat herself on his lap. "Our celebration starts with a special bottle of merlot I bought at that little wine shop in Somerville Center. Pretty expensive for our budget. We can have a glass of that here. That's before we go to your parents' and our favorite Italian – the Blue Parrot in the North End, where I've made a reservation. Haven't been there since the last time they took us." Janell whispered in his ear, "I know you like treats but I'm not going to tell you what I have planned for when we get back here."

From the desk she led him over to the settee where there were two stemmed wine glasses waiting. A small bowl of salted almonds was next to the glasses.

He stopped for a moment to take in this change in their usual routine. For one thing they never had wine at the end of the day during the week. As they sat he said, "I hope you realize this is going to change our lives – a lot. I glanced at just one of the papers in the envelope and it was about student loans for Tufts Medical School, where I've been told the tuition is $12,500 a year, plus lab costs, plus books to say nothing of where we'll live now that I'll be in school long hours probably every day."

Janell uncorked the wine and proposed a toast. "May the winds always blow favorably for us from now on. May the happiness of this very moment go on and on!" There was joy in her voice. You might think she had been admitted to Tufts Medical School. "I'm not sure it has sunk in yet that you are going to be trained at what is one of the most prestigious medical schools – certainly in this country and probably the world. I know it's going to be hard on both of us, but I am willing to do anything to make sure you can accomplish what you want in school. My job at Boston Consulting is flexible, so I can be here or there or anywhere you want."

He lifted his glass. "You are my inspiration. That's one reason – among many – why I love you." He was quiet for a moment and Janell could tell Matt was pondering things in his mind. "There's so much to plan for it almost boggles my mind: finances; the grind of classes and hours of studying; leaving you alone for long stretches; where we're going to live. Those are the big ones and then there are the little ones, like how I'm going to get to school every day since we don't have a car…"

She put her finger to his lips. "You're right. There is so much to think about. But let's not let all those details get in the way of the excitement over the incredibly good things ahead for you. Just think. We have each other. No kids, yet. Together we can do it all." With that she started to stroke his neck and the back of his head. He relaxed as Janell knew he would. Then she whispered in his ear again, "Let's not wait. I want to make love. Now."

The session was a long one and the Blue Parrott wasn't crowded when they got there for their dinner reservation around 8:30. Alex, the waiter, recognized them and sat them at a far table. "No parents tonight? Long time no see," he said. "Shall I bring you your favorite Chianti?" Matt and Janell nodded. "One last question. What's new? You both look as happy as ever."

They both smiled. Janell looked at Matt and indicated he was to take the question. "Um, lots, actually. We're pretty excited. In a month or so I will enter Tufts Medical School, so I guess you won't see much of us after that." Alex bowed. "Well, with that kind of news, the Chianti is on me. My deepest congratulations. I'll be back to take your order."

They were both quiet for a few minutes. "I guess I get to leave my job at the pharmaceutical lab in Cambridge in the next couple of weeks. Can't say I'll miss it. Thank you for understanding what will be required of my time. I've talked with a couple of other medical students and they say there's no way to describe the pressure that includes demanding long hours."

He had brought the thick envelope from TMS. As he put it on the table, she asked what else was in the package. Matt said, "I looked quickly, but noticed there are some questionnaires, a list of first year books and a schedule for initial interviews with some of the professors. Stuff like that.

What we have to decide right away is how the finances will play out. And that includes where we'll live."

They laughed about where they had lived for the past four years. The joke was they could never eat sardines, because that would remind them of how small the place was. Their miniature apartment in Somerville was convenient by subway to his job at the lab on the MIT campus. But TMS was on the other side of the Charles and so during dinner – among lots of discussion about lots of things – they decided they would have to move. That seemed like the easiest of the many questions hanging over them.

Ever the planner Janell said, "I'm not too familiar with that section of Boston, but maybe my sister Betsy can give us some help. She's a realtor and besides, she's lived all over. Actually, being in the Back Bay – if we can find a place we can afford – will be easier for me to reach my job downtown. I suppose it has to be close enough so you can ride your bike to TMS. But I'm really uncomfortable with that thought."

"Why?"

"I don't know – that old rust bucket of a bike may not get you there and back. I always worry about that. I distinctly remember the time it let you down – what was it – when the chain broke or something like that on your way to a presentation to a combined Harvard-MIT class." Matt nodded. He understood her concerns, but the rust bucket of a bike was all they could afford for now.

****

The next day with Betsy's help they combed the area on foot from the Charles, all over Roxbury and then to Dorchester. Most of the places were way too tiny – like what they had now – others were too big and every one was way beyond their budget. On day three, after looking at 15 different living quarters and near exhaustion – Betsy excused herself to check in on one more potential prospect via payphone. They couldn't hear the conversation, but the smile on Betsy's face told them something potentially good might be happening.

"I think I have good news. A friend of mine just decided to move out of her smallish basement place on St. Botolph's Street. It sounds perfect. Small, but she tells me the rent is cheaper than anything we've seen so far. I believe it's rent-controlled. Are you guys up for a walk-through?"

As soon as they stepped through the front door, they knew immediately it was perfect. Garden level with a patch of dirt where Janell could to grow a few vegetables. One bedroom with a tiny alcove where Matt could hit the books. And the kitchen was airy and light with a shallow bay window for houseplants. Just what Janell wanted.

"Before we take it, can we measure the distance from TMS? I want to make sure I can ride my bike without getting too wiped out after a full day of classes and labs, especially since I'll be riding at night three or four times a week. You've been a great, great help Betsy. But I have one last favor to ask. Can we use your car to see what the distance is from the TMS campus to this apartment?"

It turned out to be 15 blocks or two miles which was about the same distance Matt traveled now to get from their present apartment to the MIT campus. "Let's do it, Betsy. Sign us up. I don't think we can do better if we look for an apartment for another year."

Back in Somerville, Janell had that look on her face that he knew meant something was bothering her. "What's going on with you," Matt asked.

"It's a very exciting time and I love everything we've done so far. Maybe it's a small matter, I know, but I'm still worried about how you're going to get to and from school. The subway won't work. Are you sure you can ride the old rust bucket to TMS? It looks terrible. I think it's held together with all the rust. It looks like it might come apart any moment. And with no gears it must be hard on your bad leg. You know only too well what I think about bicycles." Once again she reminded Matt about the horrific bike accident her brother had in the Colorado Mountains, and the image she would probably carry the rest of her life. The image of her brother Danny, eyes closed, in the ICU in Denver General with the family gathered around. He had been in a coma for a month and they were all there to decide his fate.

Matt went to where she was sitting and now it was his turn to rub her neck and shoulders. It was a ritual they both used to relax each other. After a while he said, "Hey, my old bike seems the least of our worries. The good news I should mention is that I met with the TMS Finance Office today and my scholarship came through. Not a full ride, but with that money and scholarship help from my time in the Army, we should be okay. And besides, I've had Rusty for fifteen years. We'll need plenty of other things besides a new bike for me. It will be fine."

****

Matt and Janell made the move with the help of friends and their few pieces of furniture from Somerville fit pretty well at St. Botolph's. There was a fun going-away party for Matt at the MIT lab and lots of joshing about how you could always tell a Harvard man, you couldn't tell him much. Someone made a sexy nurse's uniform for Janell and another joker bought a kid's Halloween doctor kit with fake stethoscope for Matt. The wine flowed and when they got back to St. Boltoph's, Janell needed no shoulder rubbing to initiate a full-throated love making session.

****

Classes had begun by now and as expected, Matt was gone for long days and often into the night. Janell was concerned that Matt eat a healthy diet to keep up his stamina – and save money – so part of her daily routine was to put together nutritious lunches and dinners Matt could take with him to TMS. On weekends when he had free time, they strolled along the Esplanade and made their way across the Harvard Bridge to visit friends at MIT and the main Harvard campus. He once suggested Janell get a bike so they could ride together on weekends. But her response was always, "No thanks. You know what I think about bikes."

****

It was a few minutes after 10 p.m. on a Thursday when Matt started getting ready to leave the TMS Chemistry Lab. He grabbed his backpack laden with heavy medical texts, his class notes and the remains of his dinner to make his way to the bike rack where Rusty was waiting. He felt a light rain and so he poked around in his backpack for his trusty poncho. The cover not only held off the rain, but also the chill he felt as he crossed the street. Then he shoved off for St. Boltoph's and their cozy apartment.

After about four blocks, the rain became much heavier. In the dark the roadway looked slick, so he tested his brakes to see whether he could still stop. It was fine. His biggest problem at the moment was that his glasses started to fog up and the dim street lamps didn't seem to help much. He rounded Tremont Street and just as he got going on Copley he didn't notice a sizable water-filled pothole that in the rain looked like pavement. In he went. Instantly Rusty's front wheel collapsed and try as he might, he could not stop himself from falling to the right. It was an instinctive move to try to protect his right leg, even though it had healed long ago.

In the confusion Matt felt his glasses fly off somewhere along the street. The loaded backpack made his fall faster and when he hit the pavement he heard a sudden cracking sound. Could it be his right leg? All he could do was lay there for a few moments to try to figure out what to do next. He hoped his mended leg was intact, because the thought of going through the physical therapy again was impossible to think about. His feet were tangled up in the bike frame and wheels, but while he was still on the ground, he reached all around him to feel for his glasses. He finally gathered the strength to pull away from the bike and stagger to a standing position. He had other aches and pains but thankfully his right leg was fine. Without his glasses, which so far he could not find, he tried to assess what had happened to Rusty, his backpack, his glasses. He grabbed up the backpack to keep it from getting wetter and felt a pain in his right arm. After waiting for the pain to subside, he decided his main task at that moment was to find his glasses. It was obvious the front wheel was useless. It was bent in a double curve like a potato chip.

Since he had fallen to the right, he went over to the bushes by the sidewalk and felt around on the ground. The street lights were no help and it was awkward to be stooped over with a heavy backpack. No glasses, so he decided to make his way to St. Botolph's anyway. It seemed he was sore in lots of places, and it occurred to Matt to just leave Rusty since he couldn't roll the bike with the busted front wheel anyway. Maybe he could rescue it the next morning. Slowly, he carefully made his way on foot back to Janell.

"My God. What happened? It's almost 11:30 and I've

been panicked for the last hour." Matt knew practically word-for-word what would come out of Janell's mouth once he explained what had happened.

****

He took a cab to the TMS outpatient clinic early the next morning where the results of x-rays and a session with a friend in orthopedics showed nothing broken. Most bothersome was a big red patch of road rash on his right arm where he had gone down on the sidewalk, but some mild pain pills took care of any lingering discomfort there. Matt struggled through classes until he got new glasses that afternoon and his routine looked like it might be back to normal very quickly. Except for the subject of how he would get to school. At dinner that night Matt had pleaded with Janell to let him look at another bicycle.

"You were right about Rusty. I really believe that if I hadn't been on that old rust bucket, the wheel wouldn't have collapsed. But let's be serious. We love this apartment and couldn't move if we wanted to, so from this place there is only one way to get to TMS. The subway is six blocks away, we can't afford cabs or our own car and it's too far to walk. A bike is it. And another one – newer or maybe new, if we can afford it – will be much safer and I will have to learn to pay more attention to potholes." After a pause he added, "I know it sounds silly, but I've been riding a bicycle since I was seven. Even as an adult it still spells freedom for me – the ability to travel just about anywhere. It's part of my persona. How's that for a fancy way of saying 'I really love riding a bike.' I can't imagine myself getting around – especially in this city – any other way besides a bike." Janell said nothing at that moment, her concern still apparent.

The next morning at breakfast she seemed in a thoughtful

mood. "I've been thinking about what you said last night about getting to TMS versus the perils to your medical career. Naturally, selfishly, I don't want anything to happen to you. But I know you are cautious and that accident was just that. Maybe I can set up a 'Cab Fund' for those days when it is just too wet and cold for you to ride to campus."

They agreed to this compromise.

Yet a month later, with frequent rain and mounting cab bills, the need for Matt's new bike was urgent. It just so happened that the next day was a short lab day for him. At breakfast Janell said she would get off work early so they could take some time and shop for a bike for Matt. "Why don't we start with the bike shop I saw on Huntington Avenue the other day? I think it's called Back Bay Bikes and I think I remember they sell Schwinns," Janell said. "Good plan. But can we afford a Schwinn? Seems to me they'd be expensive," Matt responded. Janell insisted, "I've saved $250 for your new bike, so let's look in that range. I insist you buy a new one. But I do have to say that pretty soon I'm not going to be able to pull money out of various stashes like I have lately." Matt got up from the table and pulled her up too. The hug lasted two or three minutes.

Hand in hand they left their St. Boltophs apartment and made their way to the bike shop on Huntington. Once through the door, a giant sign over the cash register declared, "Small store. Small prices." That seemed like a good beginning. While the shop seemed small from the street, it actually extended way into the back with a dazzling display of all kinds and types of bikes. They wandered for a bit and then a teenager with a scraggly mustache came up to them and said, "Hi. My name is Bernie and may I ask, how did you find our shop?" He nodded as they told him they saw the store one day as they walked around getting to know the neighborhood. They lived on St. Boltoph's which was close by.

"Good. Now tell me what kind of riding you are going to do?"

Matt said he was a student in medical school and above all, needed reliability. He also said he wanted something fairly lightweight, but as a student their funds were limited, so they needed to be careful about how much they spent. Bernie nodded again knowingly. "I understand. May I suggest we start with the bikes on sale and work our way through those. I also have to mention that – amazingly – with more than 20 colleges and universities in the area, the shop gives students a ten percent discount. Why don't we start at the back and work forward? That way we will have covered about everything in the store."

They looked at Schwinn Collegiate models and Varsity models and World Sport models and many more. Altogether there were probably 100 bikes in an array of colors and models to choose from. It was getting a bit tiring. But it was pretty exciting at the same time, at least for Matt. They were near the front of the store when Bernie took them over to look at one of the more beautiful bikes they had seen in their entire time in the store. "This is one of our best values. It is the latest 1980 model and it has top-of-the-line parts and is pretty light. The bike is reasonably priced for the quality you get and with your student discount, I think it would be perfect for you. It's called the Schwinn Traveler."

Bernie said nothing as Matt went over the Traveler carefully. He lifted it. He inspected the gearing as though he knew what he was doing. The seat felt comfortable. He noted the tires and wheels seemed sturdy, unlike Rusty. Bernie went to the counter and came back with a Schwinn brochure sheet for the Traveler. "I can give you details and specs if you want. Okay? It says 'it features durable lugged carbon steel frame, with racy appearance, good quality componentry and color options. You can travel on it anywhere.' I can give you this catalog sheet with detailed specs on the wheels, gearing and the like if you want. The color is called Scarlet Flame." Silence. "What do you think so far? "

Janell spoke first. "I like the color. I also like that it looks good and sturdy without being too heavy. Now the important part – how much is it?"

To lots of people buying a bike was a fun experience. It was that for Matt too, but it was much more. This machine had to get him back and forth to medical school for four years – and possibly beyond that also.

In the end, with the sale price and the student discount, Matt walked out of BBB with a brand new, scarlet red Schwinn Traveler for $185, albeit with a stash from Janell. He was very happy. Janell was very happy. "One last thing before you go," Bernie said. He walked over to the counter and came back with a sizable sticker. He applied it on the bottom of the tube that held the seat. "There. Now you are official with the store's **BBB Boston** decal on the seat tube. Thank you very much." The bike soon took on the name Traveler. What else? It seemed to be the most natural to Matt.

As expected, Traveler took Matt safely from home to school and back all through his freshman to senior year at Tufts. The seasons changed. Matt and Janell fell into a routine. But twice a year, they made time and saved money for a romantic dinner, usually at the Blue Parrot.

In his fourth year, Matt scored near the top of his class. He excelled in biology and chemistry and started to see he might be interested in trauma medicine. That probably came from his experience in the Army. Except for a horrendous snow storm in February that lasted three days, Traveler took him to and from the TMS campus with ease. It was his joy.

****

Janell had her challenges too. Her company, Boston Consulting was growing very fast. Each year it seemed to post record growth and recently it reported to its employees that 1984 would be its best year ever. Her job as an Assistant Account Executive meant she was near the top level that women at BC could rise without too much chance – maybe any – for her to grow further. But she was determined to play a bigger role – she was shooting for Account Executive – and so she put in extra hours and extra effort. It worked.

In March, Janell got what she had worked tirelessly to achieve and now she was one of only two female Account Executives at BC. Matt was very proud of her and this time he found some extra money of his own and took her to dinner in the North End.

With her promotion came a bigger paycheck and so, for spring break in early April, they rented a car and arranged to go to the Cape and visit her friend Anna, who had a spacious house in Harwichport. Matt put down the rear seats of the hatchback they rented and managed to squeeze in Traveler. While it was still briskly chilly on the Cape, Janell buried her trepidation about bicycles and asked if she could join Matt on some of his bike rides. She asked Anna if she could borrow a bike to ride with Matt. From behind the house came a wobbly-wheeled, rust-bucket that looked and operated – as it turned out – at a lower level than even Matt's faithful old Rusty back in Boston. When Matt pumped up the tires, the rear one pressed against a rust-covered fender and he had to pull it out with all his strength to make the bike rideable. Nonetheless, it became a ritual, and Matt and Janell rode the Cape Cod Trail nearly every day they were there. Besides the creaking and clicking sounds when it was underway, the only real failure of the Anna bike was when a pedal fell off, but they somehow fixed it and resumed their daily rides.

Matt remembered riding an open-air train car as a youngster when his family visited Cape Cod for vacations. The fun part of the ride was when his father scolded him for hanging out the window with his sister. Now the old railroad right-of-way was the paved trail for two-wheelers. At one point they stopped at a trail-side marker to learn that the Osterville Railway & Land Co. (OR&L) was built originally in the 1840s. Matt chuckled at some of the special trains that ran on this very route. The sign described the Happy Train that ran from Boston on Friday nights; the Dude Train for the very rich from New York.

Rounding a bend one day, an amazing scene opened up in front of them. Behind him Matt heard the grinding of Janell's brakes as she came to a quick halt. "What is that?" Her question arose because the surface of a small pond on their right was covered in red like someone had spilled red dye over almost the entire surface. "Oh. Those are cherry tomatoes. The farmer is getting ready to pick them." Janell looked serious when Matt said, "No silly. Just kidding. Haven't you seen that before? Those are cranberries."

"Okay, Mr. Smarty-pants. No. I've never seen cranberries growing before. Why do they grow here – in water?" she asked. He directed them to another trail marker. It explained that cranberries have been cultivated on the Cape since 1816. "The farmer floods his field with water so the berries rise to the surface where they can be harvested more easily. The field is called a 'bog,' which is an impermeable bed layered with sand, acid peat soil, gravel and clay."

On they went. The present route of the trail had not changed from its early days as it twisted and turned its way to destinations in north and south transporting cranberries, seafood, and passengers. They were pleased the trail was mostly flat and took them through remote, uninhabited parts of the Cape that could be seen no other way – unless you were willing to hike for miles through thick underbrush, scrub pines, oaks and sandy footing.

One day they stopped for a picnic along the way. It was far from any structure or people and was very quiet. One jogger went by, but that was the only activity they saw that day on the trail. Janell pulled her special egg salad sandwiches on croissants from her backpack and laid out all the rest she knew Matt loved: kosher dill pickles, broccoli spears with crème dressing and a cold bottle of chardonnay. Lying back in the grass of a tiny meadow after lunch, Janell said, "I pretty well know what's ahead for you when you get out of med school. What is it? Three years in the Army to fulfill your scholarship obligation and finish your internship? But what about me, my love? I hate to give up my new position at BC. What am I going to do? And where are we going to settle?"

Up to that point – with the wonderful food, the peace and quiet, the love of his life next to him – Matt was feeling amorous. He knew she would probably never go along, but he had spotted some thick bushes up a little rise that would hide them from anyone else on the trail. That idea now got pushed aside, however, as he had to gather his thoughts about the future – where they might live and what she would do after he finished school.

Matt didn't say anything for several minutes. "For me, I'm actually glad for the Army, because I don't see myself in an office seeing patients – either as a solo practice or in a group. I'm very sure I like trauma medicine. But aside from what kind of medicine I might practice, I'm not sure where we might end up. I guess it's safe to say the Army will tell us where we'll live during my internship. I don't blame you for not wanting to give up what you worked so hard for at BC. Do they have offices in other cities?

The conversation and the wondrous peace and quiet

were suddenly, surprisingly ended by a shriek from just around a bend in the trail. They couldn't see anything, but Matt was up and running with his backpack in the direction of the noise before Janell could fully process what was going on. Dashing down the trail towards the awful sound, what he found was very disturbing. A young girl about eight or nine was on the ground with her frightened parents kneeling next to her. Before he got there, he saw blood flowing from her forehead.

"Please, can you help?" the father asked Matt as he rushed up to the scene. It was at an intersection of the trail and what looked like a narrow, sandy road. Two adult bikes lay at the side of the trail and a kid's bike with a badly bent front wheel lay across the trail away from the parent's bikes. "I'm a medical student and I will do my best," Matt responded. His immediate diagnosis was a severe cut on her head, possible concussion, perhaps a broken leg and several other serious cuts and contusions. Janell now arrived on the scene.

"Janell, there's no phone out here, so can you ride as fast as you can to that little store we saw a couple of miles back? Better take Traveler since I don't trust Anna's bike to make it – and this is a real emergency. See if you can get an ambulance to come out here. I have no idea whether it can make it down the trail, but this girl will need more medical care than I can give her here with the supplies I have. We need to hurry." The mother started to sob.

The girl was not conscious at this point, so they lifted her head very carefully and put a jacket underneath. More jackets were used to keep her warm. Fortuitously, Matt had a fairly complete First Aid kit in his backpack, but it was clearly limited given the girl's apparent injuries. He slowed the bleeding from her head wound with a gauze patch. At this point, she had not opened her eyes and her mother sobbed even harder. At first Matt didn't see that her left leg was bent sideways in a way it shouldn't be. He instructed the father to find, if possible, a couple of long, straight tree branches he could use as temporary splints.

Slowly the girl's eyes opened and widened and she asked in a very meek voice, "What happened?" As he worked on her other wounds, Matt pondered the same question. The father came back with suitable splints and Matt began the difficult job of straightening her left leg. "This is going to hurt – lots. You look brave to me, so hold on tight while I help your leg." Gently but firmly Matt worked to pull the girl's leg back to its natural position.

After a few seconds, the girl let out deep screams and Matt considered whether to stop. "Okay. I understand how much this might hurt, but we don't know when the ambulance might get here," he said hoping one would arrive – soon. A thought went through his head: this is real emergency medicine, not class or lab or books. However, I wish some of my professors were here to consult with. By now the girl had calmed down, but the general pain from all of her wounds now caused her to cry uncontrollably. He worried she wouldn't stay awake since her head wound could indicate a concussion. Her mother moved closer now and she had calmed down as well.

Matt stood and the father came over. "It was so sudden. We were riding as a family, but we were in front and Andrea was a little behind us. We hardly noticed the sandy road that crossed the trail right back there. We heard a noise and then all of a sudden we heard a loud crash and then screaming. All we saw was the tail end of one of those dirt motorcycles disappear up a hill on the sandy road. Apparently he crossed the trail and didn't see Andrea because he just kept going. But I wonder how he could not have felt anything or heard anything. I can't tell you how lucky we are to have you here."

Matt was appreciative, but was quite anxious about the ambulance. As they waited, the little girl's parents introduced themselves as Jim and Evelyn Danforth. Both were extremely worried and thanked Matt profusely.

****

Back in Boston three weeks later, Jim and Evelyn were almost teary-eyed at their home in Newton Center thanking Matt and Janell. As dinner was served Evelyn said, "Andrea's not ready to get back to gymnastics yet, but that's a small matter considering we might not have had her at all if it wasn't for you two. We are lucky. We are blessed."

The charming part was when Andrea got down from the table to go to her room. When she came back, she had a giant heart she had made with both their names entwined. Matt was touched when Andrea handed the heart card to him. "Thank you for everything," Andrea said with a big smile.

For Matt it reinforced his will to excel in trauma medicine. For Janell, it signaled her desire to have kids – and soon.

****

At Matt's graduation from medical school, both parents made an appearance. His came down from Hanover, New Hampshire and Janell's made the trek from their island home on Eleuthera in the Caribbean. Matt's sister Lydia and her teenage son Norman came up from D.C. and assorted other aunts and uncles came from all over. It was a joyful time. At a dinner that evening for all the family, the parents tapped a glass and his father stood to make a toast. "All four of us are so proud of both of you. We know Matt's had some real adversity, but you've put all that behind you, stuck with it and have our deepest admiration. So, the parents have put together – jointly – what we've called an 'After Graduation Retreat Package.'" Janell's father stood. "The package is an all-expense paid trip to our cottage on Eleuthera. You'll be entirely alone since we're headed to New York for a month. Our sincerest congratulations."

During the toast Aunt Chloe was puzzled, so she leaned over to the person sitting next to her and asked very quietly, "What is this about Matt's adversity? I know something happened, but what was it?" Aunt Mildred responded, "I don't know either. But I love your hair. Oh! By the way, have you been keeping up with General Hospital?" Aunt Mildred was known for changing the subject, but she really did want to talk about the show.

Matt stood. "Thank you – all four of you – for this wonderful treat. It has been a tough but fulfilling four years. We can assure you that Janell and I will make the most of it as a time to relax. But, we'll have to be quick about it. Since the Army provided a partial money package to complete medical school, I am obligated to serve in an Army hospital for three years, which includes my residency. I'm happy to announce – I think – that we will be moving to Lackland Air Force Base in San Antonio, which houses the largest Army hospital in the nation. I'm specializing in trauma medicine and it should be quite an experience since many of the severely war-wounded from the Middle East are transferred there."

Matt let out a small sigh. "Now on to more mundane things. The Army provides us with completely furnished living quarters, right down to the silverware. So, we invite you back to our apartment on St. Boltoph's to see if there are any items you might want before we give them to Goodwill. Even if there's nothing you want, you're invited to come see the tiny space we're been living in for the past four years."

Maybe it was the close proximity of all those people in such a cramped space; maybe it was because a couple of people brought champagne; most probably, for many, it was a needed release. What was supposed to be a casual gathering now became quite boisterous – lots of fun chatter and laughter that filled the apartment and spilled into the tiny adjoining garden. There was only one note of discord and that happened when Norman lived up to his notorious family reputation as a disrupter. He plopped himself in Matt's old leather lounge chair in the center of the small living room – foot rest fully extended and back in the prone position so that he took up a quarter of the space – and with his typical surly teenage behavior pouted and refused to get out of the chair until his mother paid Janell the $15 they were asking for it.

The party was in full swing, as they say, and Matt had to think for a few moments before he decided he needed to have a little talk with Norman. He tapped him on the shoulder and indicated he was to follow him into the bedroom. He waited while his nephew slouched into the room a moment later. "Norman. I'm going to be right up front with you. I've always liked you and hope that feeling is mutual. I'm not your father, but as I have done in the past, I'd like to give you something to think about. By hanging out in my chair like you were, all stretched out, I suppose you thought you were hurting someone – maybe your mother, maybe me. I don't know. But the unfortunate truth is you were only hurting yourself. Why do that? I don't believe there is anyone who wants to hurt you, so don't do it to yourself. Does that make sense?"

Norman hung his head. All he said was, "Um. I'm not sure how to say this." Long pause. "Oh forget it." Pause. "But yeah. You're okay. When the party is finished can you help me put the chair in my mother's van?"

Amidst all the revelry there was another tense moment – this time in the kitchen. Still curious and with no luck with Aunt Mildred, Aunt Chloe checked around and seeing no one else, cornered Janell near the refrigerator and said, "I know there was something terrible in Matt's past – his father seemed to acknowledge it in his toast earlier – but I was out of the country that whole time. I know a little, but what was it about? Is the scar on his neck from whatever happened to him?"

Janell gently pushed Chloe out of the way and got some food out of the refrigerator. "Please. We don't revisit the past. Go ask Matt if you're so interested."

A few other items besides the lounge chair were spoken for, but Matt was reluctant when Lydia insisted on taking Traveler for a test spin. Her reason was she had been thinking about commuting to her job in the District and had been looking for a bike. When she got back, she said, "I love it. How much?"

Matt acted distracted and didn't answer her right away. After everyone else had left, Lydia persisted. "I can see myself riding that bike to work in D.C. It would be perfect on the Potomac Bikeway from our house in Alexandria into the District. In good weather that is. If the Army gives you everything else, why not a new bicycle in San Antonio?"

A couple of things pushed Matt toward selling Traveler to Lydia. He admitted to himself that he had seen the list of restricted items from the Lackland hospital and among them were: no motorcycles, skateboards, bicycles, surfboards. The administration said it was for the safety of the docs and all the staff, even interns. He also remembered when they were kids, Lydia was on her bike all the time. She had a stocky build like he did and with her hair in a ponytail she would challenge him to ride out into the countryside for miles. He had to huff and puff just to keep up.

"It will be very tough for me to give up Traveler. This may be overstating it, but that bike in good measure made it possible for me to go to medical school. As they say, 'through rain and sleet and snow.' Every day." Then he paused. "Okay. I hate to, but I'll give – sell it – to you on one condition. I insist Traveler stay in the family, so when you're through with it, you have to let me know and I'll buy it back. I am very attached to that bike." After a while Lydia paid Janell $75 for Traveler and Matt with Norman put Traveler and the leather lounge chair in her van for their trip back to D.C.

****

As soon as they got on the freeway going south towards home, Norman turned on the radio to a rock station and turned up the volume. After the first two songs – "Billie Jean" by Michael Jackson and "Comfortably Numb" by Pink Floyd – Lydia decided to protect her ears and so she reached over and turned the sound down. She was surprised when Norman didn't say anything. That eased the tension between them a bit until the next song, AC/DC's "You Shook Me All Night Long", came on. She couldn't believe the lyrics. "…Taking more than her share, had me fighting for air, she told me to come, but I was already there."

"That's disgusting. Is that what you listen to all the time?"

"Mom. You just don't know. There is a solution. I need a Walkman. Why don't you get me one of those?"

"What is a Walkman?"

"They're new. Made in Japan. It's a little machine that plays cassette tapes. It has earphones so I won't disturb you. Lots of my friends are getting them."

"Well, we'll look into it," Lydia said still disturbed by

the music on the radio. "If – and I want to emphasize if – you ever get one, you'll have to earn it."

Norman did what he often did when he wanted to escape people or situations he didn't like – he reached around to the backseat for his backpack and rummaged around until he found a pencil and his trusty sketchpad. He amused himself by thumbing through it. Among the pages were dozens of drawings – of cars he liked, an ice cream sundae, an album cover for Van Halen's "And the Cradle Will Rock", a girl's puckered lips, and his interpretation of the poster for the movie "Dirty Dancing." He turned so his mother couldn't see what he was looking at.

He didn't think he wanted to do a drawing while they were on their way home. The Boston buildings they were passing were dull and gray in his mind. None of the other passing scenes were of much interest to him until he could see an auto accident some distance ahead on the side of the road. The traffic slowed way down as a result and as he studied the crash, a drawing he wanted to do came to mind. He was pretty sure the first car in the accident was a 1975 Cadillac with a huge trunk that had been flung open by the impact with a tiny French Renault. The little car was practically piggybacked inside the big car's trunk like it was hitching a ride. In his mind it was comical. So he got to work.

Washington, D.C. May 1984

Bike helps Man meet Woman

It was warm and sunny on the Saturday after they returned from Matt's graduation celebration in Boston. On her condo deck Lydia was deep into the *Washington Post* when she sensed a body opposite her. When she looked up she was astonished to see her son Norman sitting across from her since he rarely made it down for breakfast on weekends by 11 a.m. – at the earliest. It was just 8:30.

Most times it was better not to say anything, but she had a plan. "What's with you coming down so early on a Saturday?"

No response. He got up, went to the cupboard and filled a bowl with Cheerios. At the table he practically put his face in the bowl to slurp up the cereal. His only response so far was growly munching.

"No really, why are you up? There must be a reason."

"Mom. Can't you just leave it alone? I'm eating. Can't you see?"

With the favorable weather that morning, Lydia ignored her son's mood and told him that her plan was to take her newly acquired Traveler bicycle for a ride – she wasn't sure whether it would be a short spin or a long one. "I don't know how much energy I have." He was indifferent. As she thought about it, her ambition rose and so she mentioned to Norman that she might extend her range. Why not try to ride into her office building in the District? That way she could be sure beforehand of the terrain along the Potomac Bike Path and the distance from their house which she understood was about five miles. All of this mattered to her goal of commuting to the District as often as possible from their home in Alexandria. Norman only grunted as she explained not to expect her before noon. "That's if I don't have to take the Metro back because I'm pooped." Then she asked out loud, "I wonder what to wear on these commutes?"

As she expected Norman had nothing to say on this matter. But that didn't stop her from musing about whether for her commute it was better to ride into town in her dress clothes, or ride in shorts and a top, take her work clothes and then change in the office. There were men's and women's showers in her building. "Honey, do you know anything about those bags that attach to the back of a bicycle where you can carry stuff?"

"Mom, I'm listening to music. Can you stop asking me questions?"

"That's my plan. What's yours for today?"

Lydia expected that she wouldn't get any helpful information out of a 17-year-old young man, much less Norman, who she had learned from various counselors over the years had fewer communication skills than most his age and had a developing anger problem. At least in this exchange, he hadn't been as rude as he usually was.

"Okay. One more time. What's on your agenda for today. There must be something going on to get you out of bed at such an early hour. Tell me."

He sighed before saying, "I need a few bucks. Tim and

a bunch of us are going down to Norfolk to a concert. We leave about nine this morning."

So that was the reason for his early rising. Then she realized that the money he wanted gave her some leverage to ask more questions. *Who's going? Who's driving? When is the concert and when will they be home?* He was defiant at first, but then gave her some information to get the $100 he needed for gas, food and a ticket to the concert. She very reluctantly released the funds, extracting a promise to let her know when he would be back home – that day. "Do I assume you will be back tonight?" "Yeah," Norman replied as he took the money from his mother.

****

Out on the bike path – on her maiden voyage from her place at Riverside Vista to town – Lydia was surprised at the number of bike riders of all types. Quite a few young kids were pedaling along with their parents since it was the weekend. There were some jocks working out on the path and probably going a bit too fast for the kids and for new cyclists like her. A bunch of young adolescents on smaller bikes with thick tires were trying their skills at tricks, like riding only on the back wheel. Lydia rode cautiously and because of where she was on the bike path, and her slow pace, she saw things from a different perspective than from her car. The river from this angle sparkled in the sunlight. This point on the bike path had been laid out in a wide landscape of lawn with mature trees and shrubs she had never paid attention to before. It was like a park. Shortly, the path crossed a small road that came in from a busy parkway nearby. The sign beside it said, "Potomac Yacht Club, open to the public for breakfast, lunch and dinner." She remembered a pleasant dinner there a year ago with friends in town from New York.

So far she was thrilled with her adventure on Traveler. She said out loud to no one, "I love it. I love it. I love it." She was glad there were no stares with her outburst. Then the path went up a slight rise and there she saw a miniature STOP sign, just for bikes. Apparently they were to stop at a service road that led into the back side of Reagan Airport. Lydia dutifully stopped, but she was one of the few. The peacefulness in the earlier part of the path was now shattered when a Delta jet roared overhead. And then another. But she was having so much fun she ignored the interruption.

Now the path wound through some Beechwood trees and the thick canopy cut off any views. But the aroma of the trees replaced her need for scenery. Soon, however, a wide open view of the Washington Monument and other District landmarks suddenly appeared when she followed a curve in the path that took her up to a plateau. It was like a big grassy field with lots of activity: kids playing soccer at one end; touch football in the middle; and what she figured was rugby at the end closest to her.

She decided to stop for a rest and to watch the rugby. She wanted to see the game because at one time Norman had expressed an interest in playing this very rough and tumble sport. She bought him a video and several books about the game, but he never followed through. She thought maybe his interest may have come from the slogan, "Give blood. Play Rugby." That would be Norman.

She shoved off again and wound her way along the bike path until she passed under a bridge and then came to sign pointing left that said, "14th Street Bridge." This would be another first for Lydia. In all her years living in Alexandria and going back and forth to work in the District – it seemed like thousands of times she had crossed this span – she had never done it in any other way than in her own car or in a taxi. With some nervousness, because she was on her bike, she navigated her way across the Potomac, which at this point was very wide. Great views again. She had to concentrate to avoid other bike riders and pedestrians on what was now the bridge sidewalk, so she could only take a few quick sideways glances. Gliding down the other side, she had to admire the Jefferson Memorial on her left. Handsome. Bigger than she remembered. On a bike it was more up close and personal than she had ever seen it before. She had left the path by now and was on 14th Street with the stately Bureau of Printing on her right.

She stopped to decide whether to ride further into the District to her office which wasn't far from here – to fully experience her coming bike commute – or turn around and head back to her apartment. She breathed deeply and felt pretty good, although her legs were a tiny bit shaky. Just then two fit looking bike riders who appeared to be a couple pulled up beside and stopped. They had a map. "Excuse me, but can you tell us how to get to the Potomac Bike Path because we want to ride out to Mount Vernon? And do you know how far it is from here?"

Lydia pulled Traveler over to be closer to them so she could point out the route. "Sure. I've just used the bike path to come from Alexandria, which is on the route to Mount Vernon. I'm headed back that way. But you two look like real athletes, so I'll leave you after I show you how to get on the path. Someone told me it's about 18 miles out to Mount Vernon from the start of the bike path."

The man spoke first. "Do you live in Alexandria? That's interesting because we've just bought a place there. My company transferred me from New York to the D.C. office. We really love your town. Wish we could move in right away, but we're staying at the Hilton in the District until our condo is ready. Since we might be neighbors, let me introduce us. I'm Stuart Hinsley and this is my wife Laurie."

After Lydia introduced herself, it was Laurie who said today she wasn't really up for a 36-mile bike ride – out to Mount Vernon and back. Why didn't they all three ride along at a leisurely pace, if that was alright with Lydia, she suggested. "Maybe you could show us around – we only know Alexandria from the realtor's perspective and with you it would be much better."

Off they went. Lydia was surprised at how different the surroundings on the bike path looked going the other way. They admired the river, the curving path through the trees, the open spaces. All of it. Stuart remarked at how close Reagan Airport was to Alexandria. "I'm sure I'll be there a lot, going back and forth to New York. But it looks easy. Maybe I could ride my bike."

When they came to the sign on the path for the Potomac Yacht Club, Stuart stopped to ask a question. "Anyone for lunch?" So they turned into the driveway and headed their bikes around to the club's Snack Bar right on the water. What a stunning view. Somehow from this angle the District seemed almost on top of them. The Washington Monument looked like it had grown taller than Lydia remembered it from the last time she was here. They sat in the sun and talked. Stuart was a CPA with KPMG, one of the biggest accounting firms in the world. Turns out he was the new managing partner for this key office which served both government and huge business clients. Laurie had been recruited to be the executive director for Easter Seals in Northern Virginia. Their decision to locate in Alexandria was for his easy commute into the District and the proximity of the airport and because Laurie's office was in downtown Alexandria.

On the way out, Laurie stopped at a giant poster by the door which announced in bold letters the Third Annual Potomac Tinman Triathlon. Below the headline it said,

"Get ready for a half-mile swim, 25-mile bike ride and a 10k (6.5 miles) run. Lots of fun. September 25. Starts and ends right here at the Yacht Club." Laurie mentioned to Lydia that she and Stuart might enter. Why didn't Lydia consider doing it with them? "We could train together."

"I don't think there's any way I could do all that. I've run a Women's Wellness 10k, but as for the swim and the bike, those distances are way out of my reach. And besides, I only have a modest Schwinn from my brother in Boston. You guys look like real athletes."

Stuart said, "Nonsense. Your bike looks fine. What is it? A Schwinn Traveler? That should be just fine for this event. And we've got three months to train."

After riding around town for about an hour and exploring the Torpedo Factory Art Center on the waterfront, Stuart and Laurie bade Lydia goodbye with hugs. It was the start of a great friendship.

****

Lydia was back at her unit in the Riverside Vista after another 20 minutes and after a quick shower, she was so worn out she practically shot onto her bed for a well-deserved nap. It was five o'clock. When Lydia awoke it was dark. She squinted at the clock and was surprised to see it was eight o'clock, which meant she really must have been very tired from the bike ride to sleep for that long. Drowsily, she made her way to the kitchen for some tea and a bite of food. After a while it occurred to her that Norman wasn't home yet from Norfolk. Out loud she calculated the timing using her fingers. "Let's see, Norman said they were leaving at nine o'clock in the morning, which probably didn't happen knowing him and his buddies, so who knows when they actually left; it's about three and a half hours to Norfolk;

the concert was at three in the afternoon and it probably got started late and lasted two hours; then some time for fooling around, which they are very good at especially in a military town with lots of young men about his age; then the trip back here. That means they should be back here between eight and nine o'clock. That's right about now."

To await Norman's arrival Lydia moved to the couch in the living room to read her book. An hour went by and her anxiety level crept up. She pushed it back down with her reluctant knowledge that Norman has almost no sense of responsibility. And his behavior seemed to grow more quarrelsome since the divorce three years ago. Lydia had spoken with friends about the situation with Norman; she went to the school counselor; several times she had tried to talk with him about her split with Ted three years ago, but each time his eyes rolled back and he shook his head. The thought of calling to say where he was would never occur to him in spite of her repeated requests for him to do so. At eleven o'clock she became frantic. She knew Tim's parent's phone number, but it was so late. As was her habit practically living alone, she muttered aloud, "Should I call Norman's father in Arlington? Hah. My ex-husband is hardly ever of help when it comes to Norman. And besides he's probably in the throes of love-making with his new wife Pam."

When midnight came Lydia was in panic mode and so she decided to take action and picked up the phone to call Tim's parents. The phone rang and rang and then a very groggy man answered. "Hello?"

"This is Lydia Herzog, Norman's mother. I'm terribly sorry to bother you at this time of night. I understand your son and mine and some others went down to a concert in Norfolk today and I expected them back about nine o'clock tonight. Do you know anything about where they are?"

After a pause in which she could tell he covered the

mouthpiece probably to talk with his wife, he said, "Hi. This is Tim's father, Fred. Tim did come back about 9:30 tonight. I remember him talking about their adventure. He mentioned something about his friend Norman wasn't with them because he decided to stay down there for the night."

Lydia held back tears. Fred went on, "We didn't think to call you since it seemed like no big deal. And we figured your son would let you know his plans to stay over." Lydia was sniffling. "That's all I know. I have no idea what happened, but let us know if we can help. You have our number."

Lydia thanked him and went into full tears. But she quickly realized that wouldn't get the information she needed about Norman, so she got on the phone again and called her ex-husband. There was no answer the first time and when the answering machine came on she practically screamed into the phone, "Ted. This is serious. I need to speak with you immediately. Norman is missing. Call me right away."

She called again and this time a terrible-sounding Ted picked up. "What's all this about Norman?" She related his trip to Norfolk with some friends to attend a concert. She expected him back at the latest by ten o'clock. "I called the father of one of the friends he went with and that kid is home, but he said Norman decided to spend the night in Norfolk. I've not heard from him and know nothing about where he is. This is awful. What should we do?"

Ted waited a bit and then answered, "I thought you had better control of that kid. How come you don't know where he is at 1:30 a.m. on a Sunday morning?"

With that comment Lydia felt the rage she had experienced living with Ted, even with the limited contact she had with him in the past few years, all come back. "Look buster. In 17 years you have never really taken responsibility for Norman. So, now is the time. I've dealt with all his shenanigans over the years while you just stood by – and then you left us. At this point my nerves are frazzled and so I'm turning over this situation to you. You find Norman. Call me when you have information."

After she hung up, with tears streaming down her face, she muttered to herself how much she regretted turning over anything to Ted. This made the situation worse. Lydia tried again to read her book. It was impossible. She thought about calling Ted again and rescinding what seemed like her crazy move to involve him at this point. But that would just take him off the hook – once again. She couldn't wring her hands much more since they seemed raw in several places. She paced around her living room and into the bedroom over and over. It helped a little. She tried reading again, but it was useless. She never should have turned over something like this to Ted. "It's 3:30 in the morning. I can't stand it. I've got to call Ted again."

The phone rang and rang and then a woman answered. "Is this Pam?"

"Yes it is. Who is this?"

"It's Lydia.

Calmly. "What can I do for you Lydia?"

That question seemed so flippant at a time when Lydia was so overwrought that, if she could have, she would reached through the phone line strangled that woman. Fortunately, Lydia had suppressed her hysteria enough over Norman's whereabouts, so she became as controlled as Pam. "I'd like to speak with Ted."

"He's not available right now."

Suppressed rage again. "With this crisis with our son, what could he possibly be doing that he's not available to speak with me?"

There was silence and then Pam said, "I believe he's on his cell phone."

Lydia felt a touch of faintness, but shook it off. "I want to speak with him right now," she said with growing anger in her voice. "I need to speak with him immediately."

"No need to get angry with me. Norman's not my son," Pam said coolly.

Lydia quickly realized Pam was trying to make this conversation as difficult as possible, so in order to get what she needed, she decided to try friendliness. "Pam. I could use your help. Can you tell me who Ted is talking with?"

"It may be private, but I'll ask. Can you hold?"

Some time went by and then Pam came back on the line. "I asked. He's talking with the Norfolk Police."

Those words caused Lydia to shake and her tears started again. That meant there had to be some problem with Norman and her mind ranged over the possibilities. Had he been drunk and disorderly? Did he get in a fight? Had a he stolen something? Get involved with drugs? Then she realized she was imagining terrible things her son might have done—without knowing anything about Norman's situation. In a subdued voice she asked, "Do you know if he's hurt – injured? I'll hold while you find out."

Ted came on the phone this time. "He's okay, but it's a mess."

"What is going on? I need to know right now. What is the mess he's in?"

Ted started at the beginning from what the police told him. "Apparently the concert started late, I think they told me about five in the afternoon. As these things will, the concert ran long – apparently it went on for a couple of hours. At about six o'clock, again as happens in these teen concerts, a group tried to rush the stage and things started to get out of hand. The police were plentiful, they told me, but it was a pretty unruly bunch and so the police stared to haul off the 'ragers', as I think they called these stage crasher-types. They collared a dozen or so to haul them off to the station."

"So what happened to Norman?" she asked nervously.

"You know Norman and the police. This is what they told me. Before he actually got on stage, he was apprehended, but worked his way out of the officer's grip – and because the concert stage was on the edge of one of those big, high Norfolk piers – he ran and just jumped into the bay. By now it was getting dark. The officer I talked with said they spent an hour looking over the edge and into the water, trying to spot him with flashlights. Nothing. Now they were panicked, thinking he may have drowned."

"This is horrible. How did they find him? But you say he's safe?"

"Yeah. The cops finally called in the Navy. They have those huge searchlights on their rescue boats and so they scanned the area – back and forth. They searched for about an hour. Apparently Norman swam half a mile to a dock at water level and pulled himself up and lay flat, hoping not to be seen by the police. It took the Navy another hour to find him and when they discovered him, he was, according to the cop, hypothermic – shivering and shaking uncontrollably. The water temperature this time of year is about 65 degrees and he's lucky to have survived. The cop seemed to think he would be fine. He was at the hospital being warmed up under a ton of blankets when they called me."

Through tears Lydia said, "I'm really glad he's safe. What do we do now?"

"The officer I spoke with seemed pretty reasonable. There could be charges of resisting arrest, but I'm leaving shortly to go down there and see what I can do. They're not going to put him in jail or anything like that. I'll pick him up and bring him home to your place."

Lydia collected herself. "There are a lot of things I've

been through with that boy. There are many things that you don't even know about."

"Like what?"

"I know you have to get going, but just one more incident of his terribly poor judgment was about two weeks ago. Norman knows I've been trying to save money on gas and carpooling a couple of times a week. I'm actually going to start biking into work now. Anyway, he and two of his buddies took off from school in the morning, found my car keys, took my car without my permission, and were headed for New York. He never told me what they wanted to do in the city. I have my suspicions but couldn't get anything out of him. Going into Philadelphia, Norman wasn't paying attention and ran into another car stopped at a red light. It wasn't a big accident – more like a bump. You should have heard Norman describing the other driver. He said something like, 'He came running back to our car all red in the face, waving his arms in the air like a cheerleader.' Hah. Hah. They tried to talk the other guy out of calling the cops. That didn't work, so in that case, the cops called me. Needless to say the whole thing took me aback. Had the boys stolen my car? Why were they not in school? The Philadelphia police took them to the station until I could find a way to get there, since they wouldn't let him drive. I asked 'why?' Their answer was because the police took away his license, as Pennsylvania law requires of a minor not in school and with a traffic violation. Can you imagine, I had to leave work, find a bus to take me out there and then drive them back here? That was a long, painful trip with three teenage boys making light of what they had done. I was not happy and let them know it. But what did get Norman's attention was that, as I said, the Philadelphia Police took away his license."

There was no response on the other end of the line.

"There are little, niggling things too. I'm up to here with the phone calls from the school principal telling me he's not in school – again. I get practically a call a week from the school about his absences. I really don't know what to do with that kid. As you would expect, I've found marijuana in his room on several occasions. But this latest adventure seems like the worst of his bad behavior. Maybe he should go home with you. Maybe you'll have more luck with him under your parenting."

There was silence on the phone. "Um. I don't think that will work. We really don't have any room for him here. I'll bet you didn't know the school has been calling me too when he doesn't show up. So I'm not completely in the dark."

Lydia shuddered and decided to stop talking. Ted needed to get to Norfolk. She needed to get to work, even though she'd had practically no sleep.

****

Commuting by bike had become routine for Lydia, especially after she visited a nearby bicycle store and they helped her with a rear rack and panniers for Traveler. Among lots of help, a lady shop employee told her the latter term pannier was French and it meant carrying bags. She also showed her how to fold her clothes in the panniers for minimum wrinkles, as only a woman could do. And this made Lydia's commute that much better since she could now ride into the District in shorts and a sports top.

This morning she carefully packed her work clothes, as usual and as instructed, in the panniers and set off on the bike path for her office. In about 100 yards the main bike path she was on merged with a spur that came from a residential area inland from the river. Several bike riders from that section of the path practically cut her off as they stormed onto the wider, main path, but one man, a gentleman obviously, hesitated and signaled for Lydia to go first. She smiled and he smiled and she couldn't help notice his dimples and wavy dark hair. He pulled ahead of her and she lost sight of him among the many riders. She glanced at her watch. It was exactly 7:45.

It was still amazing to Lydia the stream of early commuters on the bike path. On weekdays it was nothing like she experienced the first time she took the path on the weekend. Now it was a pretty high-energy place fairly early in the morning with everyone going the same direction – and she loved it. She was out in the fresh air instead of the stuffy, crowded Metro train. By now she had noticed some regulars and so she played a game with herself trying to figure out what some of her constant companions did. Under her breath she could be heard describing the tall man on a bike similar to hers as a lawyer; the stern looking Asian man was a bureaucrat; the tidy but slightly corpulent gentleman as a banker; and the only other woman she saw was probably in the education or health field. Lydia could not help wondering what the dimple guy did in town. Then she scolded herself for playing such a game and stereotyping people.

She didn't know what to make of that part of her that regularly had her at the junction in the path at exactly 7:45 each morning, but there he was – Mr. Dimples, each time and always the gentleman. Like the first time, he went ahead of her at a fairly brisk pace. No flutters, but she kept her time at the junction the same each morning.

As she rode along one Wednesday morning, she noticed a clot of bike riders stopped in the path about where the airport road crossed. She pulled up like the rest of them and listened to the chatter, which said they were stopped for about ten minutes while a contractor moved a giant piece of equipment out from the airport on the service road. Several people exclaimed at the bad timing of the move, but generally the group was friendly and chatty, something that wouldn't have happened if not for the giant whatever-it-was that could be seen inching along the road in front of them.

Her heart did take a flutter when she glanced sideways and there was Mr. Dimples in the crowd right next to her. What a wonderful coincidence, and stopped as they were, she could get a better look at this person. Quickly she could see that the dimples weren't his only attribute. He was lean and she thought tall, although that wasn't easy to tell as he rested on his bike.

Smiles were exchanged just as they were at the junction, but this time he said, "Don't I see you at the bike path junction in the morning?" My goodness, Lydia thought, he has an Aussie accent on top of it all. In college she was madly in love with an Australian. When she first met him at a party she asked him if he was British and from that mistake she learned quickly the difference between the two accents. He had chastised her more than she expected by saying "Americans think we're all alike and we're not." No matter. Lydia had always had a thing for Aussie accents and that old "thing" stirred in her once again.

"Yes. And thank you for stopping for me."

"Of course. My pleasure. My name is Brian Tanner."

"Hi. I'm Lydia Herzog," she said, trying to suppress her butterflies. "May I ask where you work in the District?"

"You're looking at a lawyer-type who works for the Australian Embassy – who would rather not be a lawyer. One of my lawyer friends recently bought a bookstore and calls himself a recovering lawyer." Chuckles.

"That's interesting because I'm right next door in the

Education Department." Before she could stop herself she said, "So you're a lawyer. My ex is a lawyer at Justice." Obviously, Brian didn't care anything about her ex and she regretted bringing up Ted at all.

At that point the chattiness of the riders seemed to die down and they could see the policeman up ahead signaling for them to start up again.

Before shoving off, Brian said, "Call me at the Embassy for coffee some time. You can reach me through the main number. Or I can call you. Take care." And he was off. Lydia didn't start right away. She pulled aside. She needed to breathe deeply and so she rested on her handlebars for a few minutes.

****

At home Lydia liked the routine with Norman seemingly a bit more settled after the Norfolk experience. She wondered what he and his father talked about for three hours on the way back to Alexandria, but it must have done some good because she hadn't had a call from high school about his truancy for about a month. She hoped Norman was appreciative of his father going down there and working it out with the police so no charges were filed. Ted wasn't a lawyer for nothing. Norman was his usual sullen self, but nowadays he was a bit more responsive to her questions. As a result she gave him a bit more leeway in spending nights at the homes of several of his friends. However, out-of-town trips were out of the question after Norfolk.

The subtle change in Norman's behavior was a good thing. That, combined with the several contacts she had had with Brian over the past month, made life seem good – very good. Now that they had had coffee and lunch a few times, she and Brian rode together into work. He slowed down a

41

bit and she sped up and they chatted and laughed their way into the District. Her life now had a certain type of lightness to it. As she looked in the mirror putting on her makeup in the morning, her smile seemed more real and wider – if that meant anything. Work seemed fun again and she actually looked forward to the endless evaluation reports she had to analyze for her Director.

On their commute one morning in July, as they approached the Potomac Yacht Club sign, there was a banner beside it that announced in large letters, "Third Annual Potomac Tinman Triathlon Sept. 25." She had seen that announcement before. As they rode along, Brian mentioned that he was training for the Tinman. Thinking back to her visit at the yacht club with Stuart and Laurie Hinsley, she couldn't help ask why it was called a Tinman. "That's because it is a quarter of the distances of the super difficult Ironman Triathlon events put on around the world," Brian explained.

"That's right. I have heard of the Ironman. I have some friends in Hawaii who have done it. They said the Ironman was started in Hawaii. But I can't even imagine doing a two-mile ocean swim, 100-mile plus bike ride through hot, dry lava fields and then a 26-mile marathon all over the place – all together. That seems ridiculous."

"Okay, but can you imagine yourself doing a half-mile swim, 20-mile bike ride and a six-mile run? I ask because it seems to me you are pretty fit and since I'm signed up for it, maybe you could do it too. Then we could train together," Brian said with a smile.

"Funny that you ask because I met some people a while back who are doing the Tinman – the one here – and they asked if I wanted to do it also. I declined in general. My bike riding has improved commuting into town, but I'm a very slow swimmer. Maybe if we could do it over several days, but swim, bike, run – one right after the other seems out of my league."

"Don't decide now. But how about we go to dinner and discuss it over some wine?"

This was a very big step with Brian – and she wasn't at all sure if this would be a good idea. Impulsively – Lydia seemed to be more impulsive than ever lately – she said, "You know what might be fun is if we had dinner with the other people I mentioned – the Hinsleys – a nice couple who are new to the area. I know they are training for the Tinman." Then she thought better of her idea. Dinner with three other people, all fit and ready to do a triathlon she didn't think she could do, much less wanted to do, could be taxing. But she was committed – to the dinner at least.

She and Brian chose The Gathering Place, a restaurant in Old Towne Alexandria. The story goes that George Washington, when he visited Alexandria, would gather his advisors at a pub and there they would discuss strategy and tactics in their coming battles. There was also a story that alcohol at The Gathering Place fueled most of Washington's strategic moves. It supposedly was the original and seemed that way with dark wood, creaky floor and a huge fireplace at one end of the room. Even the tables and high-backed chairs were a bit rickety.

It was a very pleasant evening. As she expected, Brian got along very well with the Hinsleys and they with him. And why not, since most of the early conversation was about the Tinman. Before too much wine was consumed, Brian produced a calendar and together the four of them plotted out a training schedule for the next three months leading up to September 25. Lydia had to gulp a couple of times at what she would have to do to catch up with them. But soon the wine mellowed her and it all seemed fine.

In the classic boy-girl first kiss tradition, Brian drove

her to her Riverside apartment and she impulsively – again – invited him up. They sat on her deck admiring the views back to the District and chatted for a while about work and commuting and the Tinman. He mentioned he knew she was single from her remark about her ex who worked at Justice when they were stopped that day at the airport. And he was single too, he said. One more glass of wine and it was time for Brian to leave. She walked him to the door and before he left he leaned over and gave Lydia what she thought was a long and pretty hard kiss. After the door closed, however, she had that wide smile she recognized from her makeup mirror.

****

Because one of her co-workers at the Ed Department asked one day after lunch, Lydia had to explain what she was training for. The question probably came up because she had gone for a run during her lunch hour and her hair was wet from the shower. Lydia explained all she knew about the event. "Yes, but how do you know what you're doing? How do you know how to train," her colleague asked. She said that among the four of them training together, each seemed to have a separate strength in the various events. Brian and Laurie were excellent swimmers; Brian, because of his early years in Sydney where the ocean is a part of your life; and Laurie, because she was a varsity swimmer at Vassar. Stuart, with his experience as a Category Three bicycle racer in his earlier years, was nearly untouchable on his bike. Lydia was the best runner. She had actually competed in two Marine Marathons held each spring in and around the District. So over the three months before the event, they coached each other and the results were pretty amazing. For Lydia, the best improvement was in the confidence she gained in what would be her half-mile swim.

Later she wondered if her colleague had asked about the training because Lydia might look haggard or worn out. To the contrary, she had never felt more energized in her life. That's not to say she didn't often go home after a particularly arduous weekend training session, take a quick shower and collapse bone-weary on her bed, only to awaken in the early evening. Sometimes after she was up on those occasions, she would call Brian and he would come over. He was such a gentleman. It seemed like they would talk for hours at a time and all the while she was hoping he would hold her – and touch her. Their usual kisses at the door were wonderful, but she wanted more. One night after one of their training sessions, she went over to his place instead and Lydia wasn't sure why but she decided then to get more assertive physically. It wasn't everything she wanted, but his caresses around her breasts and stomach told her all would be well. She could wait.

It happened faster than she thought possible. Brian came over about five in the afternoon two days later and said he was tired from a 30-mile bike ride Lydia couldn't make. In the kitchen he touched her nose lightly and said, "You are beautiful," then ran his fingers along her throat. She held on to the counter. Then he kissed her tenderly and suggested they take a nap together. Norman was at a friend's house, so she thought why not? "I am really ready for that, but I need to take a shower first," she said. Brian was stretched out on her bed as she closed the bathroom door, and inside the door she said quietly to herself, "I better make this quick because I don't want him to go to sleep."

She had forgotten after her college experience, but learned once again, that Aussie men are slow, tender lovers. The wait had been worth it. It seemed they made love for hours and Brian treated her as she had never experienced sex before. He never rushed. He always stroked her in ways that made her moan – as she told him, like a schoolgirl. At one point they both sat up in bed and laughed when it seemed liked the right time to stop, have a glass of wine and then resume their lovemaking. When she got up to go to the kitchen for two glasses of chardonnay, she turned to him and said, "Sex with you is fun." Was she falling in love? Could be.

****

At about ten o'clock the next morning, she stroked Brian's neck and he opened one eye. She said, "Are you as happy as I am?" He nodded and smiled. The dimples were more prominent than she remembered them. As she sat up in bed, "How about this – I'd like to go down to the kitchen and make you breakfast. How about scrambled eggs and I'll make waffles? I've got real Vermont maple syrup a friend gave me – all of that with some fruit and fresh coffee. How does that sound?"

"Great. You are too much. Let me catch a quick shower and I'll be down. I want to help."

Lydia was at the stove preparing to cook eggs and make waffles when a disheveled Norman unexpectedly appeared in the kitchen door. She waited a bit and then asked with a note of sarcasm – which she regretted after she said it – "Another surprise early morning appearance? Where to this time? Honestly Norman, you look a mess. What's going on? I thought you were at a friend's house for the night?"

It seemed like another one way, dead-end conversation – unless, of course – he needed money like the last time when he went to Norfolk. But she tried. "Want some orange juice? I'm making waffles." Why was Norman home so early? How should she tell Norman she had a guest? It seemed complicated to explain and she thought maybe he would leave the kitchen before Brian came down for breakfast – to make her situation easier. While he looked in real need of a shower and some clean clothes, she couldn't force him out of their kitchen.

Norman noted the two place mats she had set up on the counter and moved over to one and started fiddling with the place setting – rolling the spoon and twirling the knife. In doing that he knocked over an empty juice glass and it shattered on the tile floor. To Lydia's surprise Norman went to the cupboard and got the brush and dustpan and was down behind the kitchen counter sweeping up.

Though they weren't face-to-face, she finally decided how to tell Norman about Brian by saying, "I have some news. I'm training with a friend for a triathlon. He's here…"

Just as those words started out of her mouth Brian snuck up behind her – silently – and spun her around for a good morning kiss. It was at that very moment that Norman rose up from his sweeping on the other side of the counter to see his mother being kissed by a stranger – in the embrace of a stranger – who was nude and visibly tumescent. The look on Norman's face was pure astonishment. Then his lower lip curled in anger. He dropped the broken pieces of glass and ran out of the apartment. Nothing was said then – or later.

****

Lydia checked Norman's room several times, but he was not seen all day Sunday and Monday morning he still wasn't in his room. Just before seven o'clock, the phone rang. It was her close department friend and colleague Alisa reminding Lydia that she was "in the barrel" for a big presentation and not to be late.

"Thanks, my friend. I do have a problem. My son seems to be missing."

"Oh dear. That is a big problem. You have a decision to make. Hope to see you in the office. Don't know what we'll do if you are out."

"I've made the decision. I'll be there. I'll explain later."

Since she decided to go to her meeting at the office, Lydia would call Ted later in the day to talk about this latest disappearance of their son. But her plans changed again when she got to the bicycle locker in her condo garage and there was no Traveler. She was positive of where she left it in the bike rack, but there was an empty spot where Traveler should have been. Thinking she had forgotten where she left it, she carefully examined every corner of the whole locker. No Traveler.

Lydia went back up to her apartment to call Brian to see if they might drive in together. Before getting on the phone, she checked Norman's room again, but more carefully this time. Clothes were strewn around, which wasn't at all that unusual, but it looked like he had dumped out his whole closet. A closer look revealed his big backpack was gone. His smaller school one was in a corner. On a hunch she checked the hall closet and as she suspected, her sleeping bag was gone too. It slowly came to her that Norman had taken off, but this time was it on her bike. Could that be?

Brian didn't answer when she called, so she called a cab out of necessity.

****

At 7:45 a.m. at the bike path junction where they usually met, Brian waited about ten minutes. That was all he could spare waiting for Lydia to appear and so he shoved off with a large measure of disappointment stuck in his throat. He muttered to no one, "How quickly things change."

Late in the morning Lydia called Ted on his cell

phone. He didn't pick up at first, but then he answered abruptly, "What is it this time Lydia? Another Norman safari?"

"You guessed it right, Ted. I may have caused it, but I believe he's taken off again."

"Did he take your car again?"

"No. Believe it or not, I think he took my bike."

"What on earth were you doing with a bike? How did you get a bike?"

"I bought it from my brother Matt in Boston after his graduation from medical school. You asked what I'm doing with it. Well, actually, two things I'm quite proud of. I've been riding it almost every day commuting into the District to my job. And this may surprise you, but I'm doing a quarter triathlon with a friend."

"Bully for you. Is your friend a man or a woman? If it's a man, does this have anything to do with Norman running off again?"

"Well, it could. But that's really none of your business. I'll tell you later." She felt lots of guilt. But explaining it all to Ted seemed out of the question.

"I haven't a lot of time, so give me the story."

"When I went to ride my bike to work this morning, it wasn't in the condo bike locker – anywhere. When I went back upstairs, his big backpack was gone. A bunch of his clothes and my sleeping bag. So too was about $300 I keep in a jar in the kitchen for emergencies. You know me."

"I get the picture. Maybe you did something to cause him to split once again. Didn't you tell me the Philly police took away his license? At least he had the sense not to steal your car again and drive it around without a license. And besides, the police could easily find a car. But a teenage kid on a bike would be really hard to track down. Do you have any idea where he might be headed?"

"No idea. You may remember he took a jaunt south once and north once."

Ted resisted saying maybe he would head west this time. "Doesn't he have a birthday in about ten days when he'll be 18? Not much we can do then. I say let him go. You have your life and I have mine. Maybe this will be good for him – to fend for himself. And as I said, he'll be 18 soon and then he's legally on his own anyway."

"I know, but as a mother, it's very worrisome to have your only child out there – we don't know where. This is awful. And I worry if he really can take care of himself. He's far from proving that yet." And then the guilt she felt over the Brian incident in the kitchen welled up and she started to cry.

She waited a bit. "As I said, I may have caused him to leave."

"How so?"

"Well, I've met someone I really like. As I said, I'm doing a triathlon and he's helping me with my preparation. Yesterday we did hard training in the swim and bike, and then we came back to my place to rest. Norman was spending the night at a friend's and so we decided to nap together. We're adults."

"My god, Lydia. Did Norman find you screwing? Is that why he left?"

"Just a minute, Mr. Perfect. Need I remind you what you and Pam did while we were still married? Who caught who – as you said – screwing?"

Silence at the other end.

Then, "Look Lydia. Norman's mobile. He has clothes. You say he has some money. He'll be an adult at 18 in, what about ten days? Let me know if you hear from him. Goodbye."

"Typical of you. Norman will be 18 in one week. Goodbye to you."

****

When the phone rang, Lydia jumped, hoping it was Norman. But it wasn't. It was her brother Matt saying he and Janell would be coming through D.C. tomorrow. They were taking their time getting to Texas before his internship started in the fall. "Just want to stop by and say hello since we'll be on the road for a couple of months," Matt said.

"Sure. Love to see you. What are you going to be doing traveling for that long?"

"Interesting you should ask. The Army has assigned me to visit a number of their medical facilities en-route and give them a report on their trauma centers. We'll be stopping at Walter Reed in your neck of the woods. Then Fort Benning in Georgia. They have suggested stops at other Army posts if we have time. Most are high-risk Army facilities with airplanes and skydivers and all that stuff. But we can talk about that when we get together. How is six in the evening tomorrow?"

"Great. See you when you get here. We can have dinner. Please understand I may be a bit distracted. It's about Norman. But it will be wonderful to see you both. Oh, and I have someone I want you to meet. His name is Brian."

After Matt hung up, she wondered aloud whether she should have told him – among other things – that Norman had run away on Traveler. What happens if he asks? No. Then she'd have to tell Matt and Janell all about Norman taking off on her bike. If he asks I can tell him then.

She did want to tell them about Brian.

****

At dinner in her apartment Matt and Janell had a good time talking with Brian. Lydia seemed subdued. Brian told some wonderful jokes and Matt decided his sister had made a good choice. He would tell her his opinion of him by phone later. What he wanted to tell her right there was she looked haggard and tired when he thought she should be joyful with her new relationship. She had mentioned something about Norman in their earlier phone conversation and he wondered if her appearance and demeanor had anything to do with that. There was one way to find out.

"How is Norman doing?"

Lydia sat back in her chair and shook her head slightly. She seemed to shudder just a bit when she said quietly, "I haven't been fair to Brian these past few days because Norman has me so distracted. To get it right out there, he took off and I haven't heard from him. Truth is I'm getting desperate. He left suddenly on the bicycle – your Traveler – so there's really no way to track him down. I don't know what to do." And then her tears began. Brian moved over and took her hand.

"I know you said something about Norman when we talked earlier, but I had no idea he was gone. How long ago was this?"

"Two days. Seems like an eternity. I don't know where to turn for help. When I talked with his father he practically – well no – he said straight out, 'let him go.'" The room was quiet. Then Matt said, "I've always liked that boy. We talked in Boston at my graduation party in our apartment. Remember him stretched out in my lounge chair acting like a jackass? When we talked it was about his not doing things that bring him trouble. My point to him was 'don't hurt yourself'. Did it do any good? I don't know for sure. Maybe a little. Let's face it. He's a pretty typical teenager who needs to grow up. It's easy for me to say because I'm not the parent, but I believe he will come back from this escape changed. I have confidence in him."

Lydia said, "Thanks Matt. I feel a little better."

They ended the evening with Matt again expressing his assurance to Lydia that Norman would be all right. "But you have to make me a promise. When you hear from him – and you will – let me know. And if you want, I will continue the conversation we had in Boston and add to it, if that will help," Matt said.

Virginia _May 1984_

Escape from home on the bike

His first day offered some good and some not-so-good moments as Norman made his escape from hearth and home. There was one encounter which occurred midday, that had the potential to give him some direction in this odyssey – even though he might not have realized it at the time.

Since it was early Monday morning, traffic was light as he headed south. What surprised him was how he could be riding along feeling elated for a while and then a bit later he would feel uneasy. Going south somehow felt right for this journey, but he had no idea of his real destination or of the route he would take to get there. Maybe that was it. He was free and yet at times – with no direction – he wasn't. He was gone from his mother – and her new boyfriend – and that felt good – but then it occurred to him that he couldn't go back and that made Norman feel bad. After a while he was determined to avoid the down times and so whenever he felt gloominess coming, he thought of his new favorite Olivia Newton-John song "Magic".

He couldn't figure out why he felt self-conscious singing it quietly to himself as he pedaled along, but the words made him feel good. So he kept on singing and humming the words he could remember, but at a low level.

"You know I will be kind. I'll be guiding you…you won't make a mistake." Olivia's song was so new he couldn't remember the next part, but he did know part of the last verse and it made him feel good. *"I'll come any time you call. I'll catch you when you fall."* His music reverie was halted in his first hour, however, as he was riding along through a residential section of Alexandria. He hardly noticed a man, walking his dog, who stopped to chat with a neighbor. As he did, his dog got loose from its leash, and snorting loudly, came toward Norman with what he was sure were giant fangs. God he was scared. It wasn't a big dog, but it certainly looked mean. It all happened so fast. What really bothered Norman more than anything was the slobber around the dog's mouth.

With no experience dealing with dogs while biking, Norman jumped off, grabbed the bike like a shield and shouted loudly to fend off the dog. The only problem was that the bike was a pretty leaky shield with its main triangle open in the middle, so Norman shook the whole bike at the dog, which seemed to make it only madder. Luckily by now, the dog's owner started running over, grabbed the dog by the collar and pulled it away from Norman. But Norman's heart was racing. He didn't need this. From then on, he would avoid dogs no matter what.

As he pedaled along a short while after the dog incident, it occurred to him how lucky he had been. If the dog had bitten him, the owner – or someone else – would probably have called the police, who would have wanted to see some ID and having none, would have quizzed him about where he lived and where he was going – at the least. Somehow they would have pressured him to call his mother. That was not going to happen.

He held up two fingers -- two things to avoid – dogs and cops – both four-letter words.

About a dozen miles later, if one had observed Norman as this point in his escapade, it would have looked like he had ants in his pants. He squirmed around on the seat, moved up and down, leaned way forward on Traveler's handlebars and shook a leg now and then. It wasn't ants – his butt was sore from the bike seat. So he stopped.

Where he stopped was a pleasant little park with a bench nearby which looked like it might give him some relief. He'd gotten up very early – he made sure to get up at 4 a.m. – to make his escape without his mother quizzing him about where he was going. Plus sitting in the hard saddle for about three hours was much more than he was used to – so he dozed. He actually fell into a deep sleep and didn't see or hear the park's sprinkler system kick in. By the time he awoke and went to his bike, the panniers on the back and their contents were soaked. And worse, after the soaking, they now seemed to weigh double.

Norman walked the bike for a while. By now it was close to noon and he was hungry, so he turned into a convenience store parking lot. At the door – for some security – he tucked Traveler in by three very shiny Harleys. Chrome all over them. They looked much more appealing than his lightweight bike with its narrow seat and narrow tires, and besides, you never had to pedal those babies. Opening the door he felt cool air rush out and he couldn't avoid the three Harley riders coming through the door. He said hello. There wasn't a response.

Norman hadn't given much thought to how he would spend the money he "borrowed" from his mother, but he knew he would have to spend it carefully if it was to last. He bought a bag of chips and a chocolate bar.

Outside, two of the Harley guys confronted him. The

one all in black said, "Hey skinny boy on a skinny bike. Who said you could park that kid's toy next our big boy bikes?" The one with massive tattoos came in with, "You're lucky. If that thing had fallen on any of our bikes, you'd be eating it right now – the whole bike. We don't have much to do with bicycle riders. Make sure you get out of our way – else we may have to help you get out of our way."

The two snarly riders fired up their bikes and roared off with exhaust fumes hanging in the air. The third held back and came over to Norman. "Don't pay any attention to those guys. They can be real jerks at times. I wonder why I hang out with them. So what's up with you? You look a little lost."

"Do I? I'm heading south – on this bicycle."

"Where you headed?"

"Don't know exactly. I thought about Richmond. And then after that maybe Virginia Beach."

"Good town, Richmond. It's good there. You running away – by any chance?"

"Not really. Just riding along, I guess maybe because I'm trying to escape. My mother and her new boyfriend."

"I know that one. Didn't call it 'running away' myself, but did the same thing when I was about your age. By the way, how old are you? Don't tell me. I would guess about 17. About the same age as when I took off too. I was lucky. I had someone help me. Is there anything I can do for you?"

"Ah, yeah. I need an ID. Do you know anyone around here who can get me an ID?"

"What happened to yours?"

"Some friends and I were on a trip to Philly and the cops stopped us and took my license. If a cop stops me again, I'll be in real trouble." Norman was happy to have some company but didn't want to go into detail about the Philadelphia trip. So, changing the subject he asked, "Do you know the best route to Richmond – for someone like me who's on a bicycle?"

"Sure. Oh. By the way, my name's Robbie."

"Norman."

"At times Route 1 can be pretty busy with traffic. I'd say Route 16 is your best bet for staying out of traffic – as much as possible. It's more country. I imagine it would be much better for someone on a bicycle. It can be hilly at times but most of Virginia's that way anyway. It starts right down the road."

"And it's away from cops?"

"Pretty much. You've got about another 60 miles to Richmond. For us on motorcycles that's nothing. But I have no idea how far you can ride a bicycle in a day – what? Thirty miles maybe? Sixty miles seems like a lot for one day. I don't know much about bicycles but that looks like a pretty good machine though. Is it lightweight? I see it has gears. That should help a lot. What is it?"

"It actually belongs to my mother. Yeah. It's pretty nice. It's a Schwinn – actually it's a Schwinn Traveler. I guess it's meant for traveling."

Robbie felt like testing – no maybe it was teasing – Norman a bit because he seemed so serious. He said, "How about that! You are escaping your mother on your mother's bike."

"Well if you knew my mother, you'd understand."

"Okay. I was kidding. You said you're headed for Richmond. Matter of fact, my unfriendly buddies and I are from Richmond. When you get there, I want to see if I can help you. I know a guy who can get you an ID. And maybe there are other things you might need. Look me up at the Ramparts nightclub near downtown. It's easy to find."

"Good deal. Thanks Robbie." That had been a good encounter in a day when he could use it – but there was a bit more trouble to come.

Norman got back on Traveler and by now his butt was rested so it didn't hurt quite as much. But all the wet stuff in his panniers was a drag. He rode for about an hour and apparently the extra weight caused his rear tire to go flat. After he got off the bike, he just stood and stared at the back tire with no idea what to do about it. In mechanical shop in high school where, as a section of the course, the teacher gave them a course on bike maintenance that included changing tires, Norman remembered drawing in his sketchbook pictures of girl's breasts with his friend Clay and not paying a bit of attention.

He walked Traveler for a few more blocks not knowing where he might find a bike shop. He took a chance and at a gas station and went around to the car repair bay and asked if they could fix a bike flat. With his head under the hood, the mechanic must not have heard him because he said nothing. As Norman started to ask again he heard a mumbled, "Turn right and in three blocks there's a bike shop. They can help you."

The shop owner Peter, who was also the chief mechanic, shook his head when Norman asked about fixing the flat. One look at the waterlogged panniers and Peter said that unless Norman did something about the weight, a flat would likely happen again. "I can fix the flat, but you have to fix those wet panniers," was the way the Peter explained the situation. Norman had no idea how to dry the wet clothes and a wet sleeping bag. But, overhearing the conversation about wet clothes, the owner's wife then came out from the back and said, "I can help. There's a Laundromat around the corner from here. Why don't you take that wet stuff there and dry it while my husband fixes your flat. Peter, can you get him some change for the dryer?"

This was all new to Norman. He had never touched a washer or dryer before in his life. Actually, it was easier than he thought and after an hour he was on the road again, quite pleased with himself for his dry clothes, lighter panniers and a fixed flat.

Later in the day it occurred to Norman he would have to find a place to sleep. And shower. He had a sleeping bag, but where to lay it out so the cops wouldn't find him? A motel was out of the question as too expensive. By now the countryside he was riding through was rolling hills with peaceful looking pastures. He saw horses grazing and occasionally some cows. The pastures looked inviting, but when he thought about the possibility of a horse staring him in the face first thing in the morning, that was not good, nor was the thought of resting his weary bones on some cow pies or horse buns. So he rode on.

Within a few miles he was beside a long, low fence of flowering bushes and beyond that the grass looked like it had been mowed closely, not like the pastures he'd seen before. Hollows filled with white sand dotted the landscape here and there. Then it dawned on him that he was looking at a golf course that he had only seen in passing on television. Another half mile and he came to a stately sign that announced Ardmore Country Club. Private. He was hungry and tired, but he turned into the curving drive anyway that led up to a grand building with columns in front and ivy climbing between the windows. He had never seen anything like it before. Norman wondered how he might get some food out of this place. He checked carefully and there was nobody around, so he made his way to the back of the building where a huge white tent was set up on the lawn. He saw fancy tables and chairs that sat waiting for what he thought would be some special party. He checked again. Nobody. Also waiting for the guests were several tables loaded with food but covered with plastic. Furtively he reached under and his hand landed on some cheese, and then some crackers. Those handfuls went into his backpack. Again under the plastic he managed to get out some deviled eggs, which were messy – but some of his favorites – and a bunch of carrot sticks. He looked and decided his stolen dinner would never be missed. That seemed like a pretty good meal, and not wanting to invite discovery, Norman was back on his bike and quickly headed down the driveway.

He stopped at the main road trying to decide where to settle for the night. Norman had no ideas. Then it occurred to him to turn left where he'd already been and check out what he now figured out was the golf course for Ardmore. On closer inspection of the flowering hedge as he rode, he saw a small opening and pushed Traveler through it. Why not sleep on this wonderful grass? The shadows were long at this point and he guessed nightfall was only about half an hour away, so he leaned the bike against a tree and laid out in a very soft patch of grass. Not bad for his first night – food and a place to sleep. And no cows or horses and their droppings.

When it was fully dark Norman got out the sleeping bag. He thought one of the sandy hollows – which he now remembered are called sand traps – with its gentle curves might be comfortable, but he soon learned that while sand might seem soft it is very hard for sleeping. So he moved to another section of soft grass closer to Traveler and was asleep in seconds.

At daybreak, with no shower to just step into and turn on the water like he was used to at home, his next puzzle was how to get clean – both his clothes and himself. Back up to the country club was out of the question. They'd surely find him out this time. But over to his right about a hundred feet away he noticed a coiled hose probably used by the workers to hand-water parts of the golf course. Why not? He ran the water through his shirt and under his arms and down his pants and felt refreshed. And amazingly, back on his bike his clothes were dry in about an hour of riding. And no coins needed.

He was prepared for more adventures the second day, but there was just one bad episode at midday when a car full of teenagers pulled next to him, shouted a string of obscenities and then burned rubber as they sped away. He didn't like it, but no harm done. It startled him though.

Norman's confidence was building. He felt much more comfortable on Traveler and his ability to ride longer distances. Late in the afternoon, however, when he reached Fairhaven, the roadside signs said he was about 30 miles from Richmond. It was tempting to push on, but in spite of his newfound confidence his legs said "no" and his mind balked at any more bike-riding that day too.

Dinner and shelter came to mind again.

Soon another sign said, "Fairhaven City Limits. Virginia's Church City. Population 15,800." Norman saw the truth of that sign for the next five blocks where first it was the Baptists, then the Catholics, then the Methodists, then Presbyterians and finally the Pentecostals. He joked to himself, if this kept up he may just have to ride on into Richmond. He shook his head and muttered to himself that churches were like cops and dogs – to be kept away from.

Four blocks later, however, some noise caught his attention and as he rode on he came to a sixth church whose sign was wrapped with a banner. It boldly said, "Annual Church Festival and Supper. All Welcome." He was leery, but the thought of food – maybe free food – drew him into the parking lot. Part of the noise he'd heard was from kids having fun on a small merry-go-round with accompanying calliope music and another part came from a jumping jack contest in full swing. People were having fun and it wasn't just the kids. The dads were grunting and groaning over an arm wrestling contest and several moms were singing loudly – he wasn't sure – hymns? He leaned Traveler against the church building and made his way to the buffet line.

With a heaping plate, he looked for a place at the long tables and spotted an empty chair with a lovely head of blonde hair on one side and about a 12-year-old kid on the other. The chairs were tightly packed together, but he knew he had to slide into that one chair. He discovered her face was as pretty as her hair. It was unusual for Norman to delay his eating any time, but for several minutes he couldn't pick up his fork while trying to steal sideways glances at the lovely girl next to him. He thought about it but couldn't seem to come up with a smooth way to introduce himself, so he just gulped and said, "Hi. My name is Norman. Can I ask yours?"

"I'm Melinda. You haven't eaten your dinner. Is something wrong? I haven't seen you before – are you from around here?"

Now she was asking the questions and Norman wasn't quite sure how to answer. "No. No. I like the dinner. It's great. I should say I'm sort of from around here. Actually, I'm passing through. I'm on a bicycle. Is that alright?"

"Yeah. Great. On a bike. Hmm. Where you staying?"

Back to more questions. He was stumped about how to ask her name a moment ago and now he was in the same position to answer her question. "Um. That's a problem. I don't really have a place to stay tonight." He hated admitting that fact to her and not wanting to sound too much like a bum, he offered, "But I go on to Richmond tomorrow."

"I want more corn. Do you need anything? Let me think about where you could stay tonight while I'm up," and Melinda turned to leave.

He had no idea what her fragrance was, but in getting up she had to come close to him and the aroma caused him to put his face in his hands. He quickly looked up, however, to follow her toward the food line. He had never seen a more perfect shape. Melinda couldn't be this good. Thoughts of ditching Richmond came to mind. Why couldn't he just stay here? Fairhaven was small, but he was sure he could be happy with Melinda.

When she left to get more food, that was a lot for him to handle, but when she came back her shoulder brushed his and he was totally embarrassed to feel a tightening in his shorts. Norman would not have been able to stand up if he had to. "Hi. I'm back. I noticed you didn't have one of Fairhaven's Famous Double Chocolate Brownies, so I brought you one." With that she plunked down a hunk of chocolate the size of a man's thick wallet. "Okay. So you're from around here, going to Richmond on a bicycle, but tonight you don't have any place to stay. You can't stay with us at the parsonage because my cousins came to town for the Festival – see the six of them over there – and they're filling up our place. But I have an idea we can explore after dinner. I have to get up right now, but wait over there for me."

The anticipation was killing him, waiting to find out her idea, but he stood patiently over by Traveler as she made the rounds of greeting her cousins and a dozen other people. He couldn't take his eyes off her. Melinda practically glided between clusters of people and her smile made him hurt.

Finally she came over to Norman and took him by the hand. "C'mon. I have a hidden place to show you." He wished she hadn't said what she said or done what she did just then, because there was another stiffing in his shorts. He was glad when she led him around the front of the church to a side door, because nobody could see his problem.

Inside the sanctuary was dark and silent and musty. Was that aroma from the old Bibles or maybe the pew cushions? Never mind. He felt he was doing his duty to glance at the huge stained glass window above the alter. But that small,

small touch of religiosity ended when she said, "Follow me. I'm going to take you to a place where I go when I need to get away from everybody." With that she led him up a narrow flight of stairs. Even with his very limited church knowledge, he did know these stairs should lead to the choir loft.

At the top of the stairs he saw three ascending levels of chairs and over in the far corner was a section with a low wall surrounding it. They climbed to the upholstered bench there and she said, "Will this do for a place for you to sleep tonight? It's not luxury, but I've slept up here myself – as I said when I want to get away from everybody." His imagination grabbed that one and he could see her curled up on the bench – beautiful, angelic maybe – in her sleep. Now by this time Norman had been – not exactly an emotional wreck – but in a good deal of turmoil about how to proceed. His imagination was taking over and that meant his body and part of his mind wanted to grab Melinda and put in practice what over several years had been only sexual fantasies. But then another part of his brain prevailed and they just sat on the bench.

He was confused. Could he hold her hand again – on his own? He tried and it worked. Could he get up the gumption to kiss her? He tried and she resisted – nicely. The ultimate would have been to caress her lovely breasts. But he didn't have the nerve for that, so they just talked.

Melinda had lots of questions. Why was he on a bike? How far was he riding? Where was he headed? How long would he be in Fairhaven? Norman's answers helped to calm him down.

Finally she got up and said she had to go over to the parsonage, "To at least make an effort to socialize with my out-of-town cousins – else my father will scold me. But I'll try to make it back up here later if I can."

"Sure. That would be great." Norman ached.

****

When he woke up late the next morning, he felt terrible. Had Melinda been there and he was so sound asleep she couldn't wake him? Had her father suspected what she was up to and stopped her? Had she not been interested? All he knew was they had not been together again for whatever reason. He was desperate to know, so he put on his clothes and went over to the parsonage wondering what he would say or do. A woman, who Norman assumed was Melinda's mother, opened the door.

"Hi. I'm a friend of Melinda's. Is she here?"

Sternly, "I don't know who you are, but no, Melinda's not here. She's in school."

As he backed down the front steps, "Thank you. Will you tell her Norman was asking for her?"

He made his way over to some steps where he had left his bike the night before. He was in bad shape. If someone had taken a picture of him at that moment, it could have been a poster for devastation, dejection, rejection. Sad. Head hung low. Face in his hands. Finally he looked up and implored his non-existent audience, "Of course she would be in school at this time of day. Where else would she be? What should I do? Should I wait for her? What if she wanted nothing to do with me? Maybe that's why she never came to the choir loft."

After another 15 minutes of misery, Norman didn't exactly peel rubber leaving the church and Fairhaven but the bike had probably never been ridden faster – not even when his mother was training for her triathlon on Traveler. He did learn he could practically race the bike. Norman covered the remaining 30 miles to Richmond in a little over three hours even with a lunch stop.

He hoped to find Robbie.

Richmond June 1984

So much to learn

After Fairhaven Norman got back on Route 1 at Saybrook. Soon the backwash from an 18-wheeler nearly knocked him off the road, but his bike handling had improved enough that luckily he was able to stay out of the ditch beside the highway. This wasn't like Route 16, though, which ambled along through the countryside – now he was in the swirl of big trucks with lots of cars and buses. He could feel the noise, the faster pace and the congestion. It meant he was approaching Richmond.

Before actually tackling the big city, he pulled into an old-style milk bottle-shaped building called "The Shakes." He was intrigued by such a display, the likes of which he had never seen before. Inside he learned this spot had been a tourist attraction for 40 years and so he had to wait a bit. Cautious with the precious money, he finally ordered a Bumbleberry Shake and a Monster Burger. He felt that would nicely satisfy him for both breakfast and lunch.

Glancing at a wall payphone, a sudden thought came to him as he waited for his food. He knew his mother would be worried about where he was and what he was doing. But there was no way whatsoever that he could bring himself to

69

call her. If he made a call, he could imagine practically every word she would say. He didn't want to hear any of that. And if he told her where he was, he wasn't sure she wouldn't call the cops.

No phone call then. But he supposed he should make contact with her some way. A letter came to mind – one with no return address. He'd never written a letter in his life and besides he had no pen and paper. But if he did write he imagined what he would say.

"Dear Mom. I know I left without telling you anything. It may seem strange, but I was really upset that morning to see your boyfriend suddenly appear in the nude and grab you like he did. But it's more than that. I know I never was the son you and Dad imagined. Really, things got worse after the divorce. I know Dad left us, but with you I felt more controlled than before when Dad was at home. I felt controlled by you, by the school, by the cops. I think Dad understood me pretty well, but not completely. I know I was often a pain in the ass, but when I thought about it that gave me some control. Honestly. Being that way has advantages. You were never sure what I would do. I want to be appreciated. Love, Norman"

As he went out to pay Norman couldn't help notice the cashier. His heart stopped for a moment at her blond hair as he fleetingly thought maybe it was Melinda. This place was close enough to Fairhaven that she could have a part-time job here. He had to stop and look away. But after that initial rush, he was glad she wasn't. Her name tag said, "Norma."

At that point he felt he needed to lighten up, so he said, "Hi Norma. My name's Norman. I'm looking for a nightclub called 'Ramparts' in town. Can you tell me how to get there?"

The Norma-Norman thing didn't get any response. Instead she flatly said, "I think it's in the Shockhoe Bottom section right on the river. I've never been there myself, but some of my friends say there are several nightclubs in that district. Not sure the route you should take to get there."

To be helpful Norma got her supervisor who when she learned he was on a bicycle said, "Whoa. That's a different story. What are you doing, boy, on a bike? Never heard of anyone riding into Richmond on a bike. Crazy." After thinking about it, she eventually suggested he go right down Route 1 into town, and eventually to Shockkoe Bottom. "Should I write it down for you? Not sure of the address for Ramparts, but once you're there at the Bottom you'll find it."

He wasn't sure why he thought it, but his mind's view of Richmond was that it was a smallish city. But that idea was changed when he stopped along the highway to take in the view of Richmond in the distance. This could be more exciting than he expected. Looking carefully, he thought a quick sketch of the contrast between the dozen or so needle-like sharp buildings rising out of the soft tree canopy might be interesting. So he stopped right where he was and got out his sketchpad. In a few minutes he had what he wanted and it would remind him of his entrance to the city where he might settle down – for a while at least.

He rode on with a quicker pace toward his river destination dodging cars, trucks, buses and pedestrians. He was the only bicycle rider along his path. He did have a little scare at a busy city intersection when he started before the light was green and a car swerved to miss him. A policeman yelled at him, "Hey kid. That's the way they make angels." He hurried on. No more of that.

Norman had a sense of relief when he finally jockeyed his way through downtown's diagonal streets and arrived at the river north of Ramparts, according to a passerby he asked. The expanse of the slow moving river seemed so calm in comparison with the hustle of the city. He quelled the feeling that he was home – where he could get off the road, at least for a while – where he should be. Part of that feeling could be filled in by what he found at Ramparts.

What caught his eye was a 20-foot-high sculpture on a little rocky island out in the river with what looked like a giant bicycle wheel. Strange. He studied it for some time before figuring out what he thought it meant. A closer look made him realize – because he'd seen them out in the river upstream – that the L was made of red and white river buoys stacked up; the big O was the bike wheel that he noticed first; two kayaks made the V with their bows pointed down. It was hard to know what the E was made from and whether it was actually an E. Straddling Traveler he asked a couple standing beside him, "What is that all about?"

"It spells L-O-V-E."

Norman was not at all familiar with love. He thought maybe some day he would figure it out, but for right now, for him, love was off in the cloudy distance somewhere. Another mystery he didn't want to take time to think about. But he wanted to ask the couple anyway, "So why is the word love spelled out in the river with some stuff that doesn't make sense?"

The woman answered, "I think they're trying to do two things – remind us of the state's slogan 'Virginia Is For Lovers,' and tell us about how active – sports-wise – Richmond is. The buoys are for the kayaks going through the river rapids you may have seen; you should know a bicycle wheel since you're riding on two of them; and the E is spelled out with backpacks to tell us there is good hiking just a short distance from town."

He wondered if he should sketch what he considered this awkward sculpture stuck out in the river. He looked it over and decided to move on.

"Hey, thanks," he responded. And Norman was off. In another few blocks he almost missed Ramparts on his left because his eye was drawn to an old watercraft tied up a few blocks down river. He stopped momentarily to look over at Ramparts and make sure he knew where it was. He noted it had a refined marquee and the changeable letters said, "Amy Through Friday." He wasn't sure what that meant, but he didn't want to go in there quite yet. It was only three o'clock. Somehow the old river craft fascinated him and so he pedaled down to it and leaned Traveler against a piling. There was an a-frame sign by the piling that announced, "Daily River Tours at 9 a.m. and 1 p.m. on the Historic River Belle. Two hours $15."

Although that kind of money for a river tour didn't interest him, he was intrigued by the fancy woodwork on the upper roof, so he took his time walking along the length of the boat admiring the old-fashioned windows and doors and trim. On the bow he noticed that the words "River Belle" were carved in gold letters. That impressed him. Parts of this boat – especially the decorative trim along the little house sitting on top and the carved name on the bow – he had to sketch. He had been working at it for about half an hour and was lost in his work.

As he started to put away his sketchbook, he thought he imagined it when he heard a voice from above say, "Hi there. I saw you admiring my boat. I saw you sketching it. You must like it. Why don't you come aboard? I'd love to see your work. Just push your bike up the ramp and it will be safe." He looked up to the little house three levels up – he thought it was called the wheelhouse from a book he read one time – and saw the voice came from a woman leaning against the railing. Was she the captain? Could she just invite anyone on the boat?

Surprised, Norman did as he was told. He could at

least find out if she was the captain. On the deck he could hear someone above him coming down old wooden stairs. He had always had a tough time figuring out people's ages, but when she arrived at the bottom of stairs, there stood a stunning woman he thought was about 30 in a low cut tank top that left a bare midriff. Very attractive with a thick dark braid over her left shoulder and tanned skin. He had difficulty – because of the distance between them – not being caught moving his eyes between her breasts, her bare tummy and her athletic-looking legs. He concentrated on her nose as she said, "Hi. I'm Ricky. Welcome aboard. I see you're on a bike. Does that mean you live in Richmond?"

He had to take this slowly. "Hello. I'm Norman. Just got to town. Yeah. I really like your boat."

"Thanks. I was just about to go for a run. But you look really interested, so I would love to give you a tour – of the boat. How does that sound?"

So off they went. She chattered away as they went toward the bow. "This is truly a historic boat...built in 1860...it was used to transport tobacco and people up and down the James River for over 80 years...I'll show you the hold where they packed in the tobacco in a bit...my brother and I inherited Belle from my father when he passed away last year...Eric, my brother, and I are co-captains." That answered one of Norman's questions. "My father rescued this old beauty from a boat yard about 15 miles down the James...that was 20 years ago...a lot of the woodwork was rotted, the brass fixtures were terrible and the engine had to be replaced...he spent about a year and a pile of money to bring it back and convert it to a tourist attraction."

Then she took him down some very steep stairs to the cargo hold. It was dark and dank. "Do you smell the tobacco after all these years?"

On the way back up he followed Ricky and much as

he tried, he could not take his eyes off her tight shorts. He thought those must be running shorts to go with the tank top. It made him embarrassed but didn't change his sight line. He hung back for a slight bit, but she admonished him to keep up. He did as he was told because he began to anticipate climbing more stairs behind her. They went up to the wheelhouse where he admired the old steering wheel, all polished brass and dark wood with spokes just like pictures he had seen in a book.

"Our engineer actually runs the boat from up here. As captain, I greet all our passengers – not in my running outfit like I have on now – as they come aboard on the main deck and make sure they are having a good time. I'm responsible for the crew of five people. Eric captains the nine o'clock run and I do the same for the one o'clock. My run is quite interesting because we serve alcohol in the afternoon and sometimes passengers start having a little too much fun." She paused. "That's about it for my personalized tour for you, but I do want to show one last thing that's pretty special."

She led him by the hand along a narrow deck to one of the attractive doors he admired from below when he was on the dock. There was a brass plaque on the door that read, "PRIVATE." He couldn't see in because there was a fringed shade covering the window. When she unlocked the door, they both stepped into a small parlor with an adjoining bedroom. It was very attractive and snug. His nose told him the aroma was a mixture of leather, old varnish, tobacco and the apples he saw in a bowl on the table. "This is where the captain lived when the Belle was in its heyday moving cargo and people on the river. It is pretty much as the original owner – who was also the captain – designed it. According to the records we have found, he would live aboard for a month at a time and then go ashore and join his family in Richmond. Do you like it?"

Norman couldn't respond to her right away because he

was taking in the old leather chair, tiny desk with a bookcase above and old-fashioned kerosene lamps. He walked around and admired about a dozen prints of early Richmond on the walls. He wandered back to the bedroom which seemed more of the same – rich, old furnishings like the parlor but with a bed taking up most of the room.

"Sit." And she pointed to the leather chair. "Tell me about yourself. But before you do that, I want to see the sketch you made of my boat."

"Actually, I only do these little drawings for my own pleasure. I never give them away. I will let you look at them only if you'll give them back."

As he handed it to her, she sat on an old wooden chest and leaned forward, elbows on her knees. Norman averted his eyes from what he could see of her full breasts. "You are good. My brother likes art too. Where did you learn to do this kind of work?"

"Art was about the only thing I liked about high school. As I said I do sketches of things that interest me. It's kind of an escape for me. But thanks for the compliment."

He felt a little shy. This woman was older. Certainly not his mother's age. Maybe ten years younger – as he thought before – maybe 30. Maybe younger. Should he tell her he was escaping home by riding his bike down to Richmond? Escaping his mother? He didn't know where to start but the words just started coming out.

After relating some of his adventures, he said, "On my way down I met Robbie. He kind of came to my defense when two of his friends harassed me a bit. I told him what I was doing. We talked and he suggested I look him up in Richmond when I got here. I haven't found him yet. Don't know his last name."

"You won't have any trouble finding Robbie. He's kiddingly called the 'Mayor of Shockhoe.'"

"Why is that?"

"You will find that Robbie knows just about everybody up and down this waterfront. Yes, there are two other nightclubs on this street, but his is the main one. He's done very well. He's always helping people, so it doesn't surprise me he would offer you help. Let's say you get a job and you plan to stay – he's a good guy to have on your side. By the way, where are you planning to live?" She got up and went over to a cupboard that hid a small refrigerator. "Oh, I'm sorry not to be more hospitable. Do you want a beer?" He refused. "And I'll ask again, do you have a place to stay?"

By now Norman was beginning to feel a little looser. "So far, I've slept on a golf course and in a church. How's that?"

"That sounds terrible. Are you planning to ask Robbie for a job?"

"As I said, I haven't even seen him yet. But I guess I'll need a job pretty soon before my money runs out. Should I look for a job with Robbie?"

"He's always got a lot of things going. I don't know, but it's not a bad place to start – at Ramparts. I have a thought. Once you meet Robbie and find out what's going on there, you'll need a place to stay, especially if he hires you. What I am thinking is, why don't you use this old suite until you get settled? It's pretty comfortable. And you could just walk to work. Leave your bike here."

"That would be great, but I can't do that. I hardly know you." He felt foolish after saying that.

"Look Norman. When someone offers you something like this," and she swept her arm around the room, "don't get all shy and boyish. I can tell by your eyes that you like this apartment. And I like you. It's time to go." And with that she got up leaned over his chair and gave him a kiss on the lips. "Let me know if you need the place. Just leave a note on the door downstairs if I'm not here."

****

Norman was still a little unsteady trying to figure out what happened with Ricky when he finally got to Ramparts up the street. Inside it was dark so he had to take a moment to let his eyes adjust. He had three first impressions: it was much bigger than it seemed from the street; it was dark; and it was mostly deserted at this time of day. The bar was straight ahead with table seating in front and on the left. Over to the right was a stage with mics and sound equipment set up. It looked like about 100 people could be seated, mostly in informal rows for the show. When he got there the bartender had his back to him, but when he turned around Norman asked, "Excuse me. Do you know where can I find Robbie?"

"He's not here now. He keeps his own hours, so we're never sure when he'll be in. Is your name Norman, by any chance?"

"Yeah. How did you know?"

"Robbie wasn't sure, but he told us you might be in one of these days. You met on the road?"

"Yes. He said to look him up here. I asked him for a favor."

"Robbie said that when you got here, we were to take you to Penny in the back. She pretty much runs the place. Come this way."

Down a hallway – stacked with boxes, past the men's and lady's restrooms and a storage room – they kept going until they came to several offices with one door marked "Manager". After a gentle knock, the door opened to a spacious office. Norman saw neat stacks of papers everywhere, a big desk and behind it a tiny woman. "Hello. I'm Penny Lum. Robbie thought you might come by. Have a seat. Robbie didn't have much to say about you except you seemed like a nice young man and you need an ID. Tell me a little about yourself."

Norman was not expecting an interview – in an office. Penny was Asian, as far as he could tell. His Alexandria high school – big as it was – had one Asian – a girl – whose father was with one of the embassies, but he never spoke with her. The similarity he saw was that neither that girl nor Penny smiled much. All business. He went ahead telling her of his experience with Robbie; that he was riding a bike; he liked Richmond; and he needed an ID. "I will be 18 next Tuesday and I don't have an ID. Can you help with that?"

"Robbie did tell me you had taken off and left your mother. Maybe it's none of our business – I say 'our' because Robbie is in this too – but have you called her? He asked me to ask you if you had." Norman shook his head.

"Getting you an ID is easy, but we'll only do it on the condition you call her today. Is that a deal?"

"I will try to get her a message. She's hardly ever at home, but somehow I will tell her I am fine." He did not want to tell his mother where he was and since that wasn't part of the deal he accepted readily.

"Okay. Now, have you ever worked before?"

"No. But I want to. I gotta start somewhere to get experience. I need someone to take a chance on me – to get started somewhere – else how do I get experience?"

"How much do you know about Ramparts?"

"I talked with the lady at the boat – what is it – the River Belle down the way. She said Robbie was a really good guy, that Ramparts had a lot going on and it had good business."

"That's a start. Probably what she meant by 'a lot going on' is that we have a concert tour coming up very quickly. Ramparts is all about country music and Amy – her name is out front – is quite a star. Each year we take her on a summer and fall tour to several cities in a southern swing. Not the major cities like Atlanta or Miami or Dallas – but secondary cities where they go nuts for her. She draws big crowds where we tour, which this year includes places like Columbus in Georgia, where the 10,000 soldiers from Fort Benning all fall in love with her. Happens every time. This year we've got something pretty exciting planned before the concert down there. Tallahassee, Florida is good too because of all the service people – Air Force and Navy nearby in Pensacola. Big, big crowds. Algiers is a little town directly across the Mississippi from New Orleans. Because of the connection with jazz in that part of the country that concert will be little different from the others that are pure country. And Laredo, Texas is all about country music. Amy is due to pick up a big award there a couple of days before the concert. That town is very good for us, always has been. How does all of that sound?"

That was a lot to take in. "I love country music."

Penny got a file folder out of her desk. "We actually start with a 'Send Off Concert' right here in Richmond, which is coming up very shortly. We're hiring for that and the overall tour right now. The home concert might be a good place for you to start – to find out whether you like what we do – and we find out what you can do." She thumbed through some papers and said, "The openings I have are: Ticket Takers. Sound Balancer. Assistant Equipment Manager. Security detail. Truck Mechanic. Any of those sound interesting to you?"

"Well, I know I couldn't do any of the technical stuff like lighting or sound. And I'm not a mechanic or big enough for security. What does the Assistant Equipment Manager do? That sounds interesting to me."

Just then there was a knock on the door. Penny excused herself and left the office.

That left Norman to exult in the fact he may have a job and contemplate what kind of job it would be. A job

– in the music business. What could be better? He loved most kinds of music. When Penny returned they settled on the Assistant Equipment Manager position. She had to check with Rudy, the show producer and tour manager and Robbie, but Norman was told he could pretty much count on it since she would recommend him for it. "I'll know for sure tomorrow. Check with me about eleven tomorrow. We can talk about who you will be working for in the equipment section and what the job entails. I know you'll want to know about wages and there's some paperwork to deal with. Last thing. I think it would be a good idea if you stopped by for one of Amy's shows so you can begin to get a feel for the entertainment we provide – at this club and on the tour. Here are a couple of tickets in case you want to bring a friend. You can use them for tonight's 9 p.m. show. By the way, where will you be living?"

"Oh. It's not final, but I'm pretty sure I have a place. Thank you for everything." And with that he bolted out of Ramparts and on down to the River Belle. He sprinted the three flights of stairs to the wheelhouse.

Inside, after he excitedly told Ricky about his "pretty sure" job with the Ramparts Tour, she came over and took both his hands. Her strong kiss on his lips was amazing and when it was finished she said, "That's my congratulations for your new job. Okay? And now you have a place to live too."

Norman was overwhelmed with all that was happening and couldn't speak at that moment. He sat back and when he had collected himself, he told her that – besides her wonderful kisses – he did have another way they could celebrate if she wanted. "I have two tickets to Amy's show tonight. Would you like to go?"

****

81

Later that day Norman left the River Belle and poked around in another part of downtown until he came to the office where Penny told him to go for his ID. Turns out it was a county office and his ID would serve as government identification as was often required. While he waited he filled out the questionnaire. Hair: sandy; Eyes: blue; Height: 5' 10;" Weight: 155; Sex: M; Date of birth: 6/14/66. He declined being an Organ Donor. Then they took his picture. When the card was ready about ten minutes later, he couldn't help looking at his photo. He kind of liked his smile. Should he show his shiny new ID card to Ricky?

****

After the Amy show they headed back to River Belle about midnight and Ricky said she would accompany him up to the apartment, give him the key and get him settled. Once inside the apartment he was excited but tired and the bed looked awfully good. Ricky excused herself to use the bathroom and Norman sat down on the bed. "Don't lie down," he said under his breath, thinking back to what happened with Melinda. Norman didn't hear the bathroom door open but could feel the bed move when she climbed on and came up behind him, put her arms around his chest and started to nuzzle his neck. What really charged him up was when she took her braid and tickled around his forehead and face. All he could manage was, "God, you are sexy." He glanced down and the stiffening in his pants was obvious.

She got up, pulled him up and they embraced. More, deeper kisses. He was a tangle of emotions as she said, "I better go." How could she not feel what was going on with him below? Suddenly he struggled to hold back the convulsions in his midsection. It was embarrassing and got worse when he felt the warm fluid running down his leg.

"Don't worry," she said. "We'll have plenty of time to be together – if you want. See you tomorrow?"

****

At eleven he was at Penny's door and when he knocked she came out and said, "Robbie is in his office and would like to speak with you. Two doors over."

Inside, Norman saw a plain office with furniture just a bit nicer than Penny's. Robbie greeted him with a handshake and a hearty, "Welcome to Richmond. Please have a seat. Well, I was pretty sure you would come by. Even though it's only – what, two or three days ago? – it seems like a long time since we talked in Fairhaven, but I'm glad you made it – bicycle and all. I asked my guys to make you welcome. And I understand you're been talking with Penny about joining us to work on our Amy Tour. That sounds good."

Norman, like an attentive student, was taking in everything Robbie said. "We want it to work out for you and for us." Then he got serious. "But I have to tell you – this is a rough business. You will work very hard, but we feel confident you can do that. But beyond work, believe me when I say there will be a lot of temptations along the way. There will be lots of women hanging around. They go crazy for Amy's Wave band members. And booze. But those you'll have to learn to handle and I expect you to do so. But drugs – now that can be a real problem. There's almost no way to control it in this business. If you want it, everything will be available. But don't get into it. Maybe a little weed now and then won't hurt anything, but the hard stuff will ruin your life. There are enough situations and people out there trying to bring you down – defeat you – not just you, but all of us – so don't help them – don't help them by defeating yourself. And that's what drugs will do. Comprende?"

83

****

Early Monday morning Norman rode Traveler about 15 miles out to the Richmond International Speedway and reported to Rudy, the shows' producer and tour manager. Behind the enormous stands Rudy showed him the two equipment trucks where he would be working. They were filled with stage risers, cables and fixtures and lights and sound equipment and more. "Your job – may I call you Norm? – is to help set up all this equipment for the tour performances and then after the show is over, take it all down and store it back in these trucks. We go from venue to venue and do it all again. Your actual boss will be Gus, our Equipment Manager, who you will meet when he gets here in about an hour. Gus can tell you much more about the procedure for setup and take down. From what Penny told me you've been assigned as his assistant."

Norman asked why the concert was at a place like the speedway instead of a more usual concert location. Rudy explained that as the producer it was his job to bring some drama – some surprises – to the show. "Amy's a total professional, but it's up to me to bring new ideas to the shows. It wasn't terribly hard, but I had to talk Robbie into having the Send Off Concert, not in the usual places like the amphitheater, but someplace entirely different, like the speedway. Think about this: these stands hold 20,000 people. Much more than any concert hall or outdoor amphitheater – at least in this part of the woods. We're selling a combined ticket – the Formula One races in the afternoon followed a short time later by the concert. The tickets are $200 each for both the races and the concert. It's a one-time deal and it's sold out. After he calculated what that amounted to, Norman just shook his head.

Rudy then took him around to the actual track where

the stage would be set up. "The immediate challenge for you and Gus is to do practice set-ups before the actual event. The reason is that you only have one hour between the last race and the concert, so you will really have to know what you are doing. Guaranteed you will earn your money. But Gus is very good at what he does and he will work with you to get you up to speed."

Norman looked up at the stands. He had never seen so many seats – then he remembered the time his father took him to a Redskins game one time. He thought someone told him once that that stadium holds 50,000 people, but this looked as big. He never thought to ask his father about the size of the other stadium.

When Gus arrived, the real work began. "We have to time this exactly. Drive the blue truck around to the marks I've made on the track. See how long it takes. I'll follow in the other truck." Did Norman have to tell him that he didn't have a driver's license? No need right now. Wasn't this private property and he could drive all he liked? But what happens if Gus assigns him the blue truck for the tour?

Norman maneuvered his truck precisely to the chalk marks indicated and hopped out. He reported to Gus that his trip was three minutes and forty five seconds. "Just okay," was Gus' response. It was hot inside the box of the truck as Gus took him through every piece of equipment. "There is no way the two of us can set up the stage and the scaffolding for the lights and sound and the other equipment by ourselves in the time we have. So I've hired some extra hands – for both the practices and the actual event. I do the same thing sometimes on tour. So we'll have help. They should be here any minute and then we can begin the practice. We'll time it again, but for this first time I don't expect we'll hit the mark."

In fact, they did two practices that very day. Neither

went according to Gus' satisfaction. In the first rehearsal
some of the light hangers were backwards and the stage
creaked under foot. But it got a little better the second time
and they had more – or maybe a couple more – rehearsals
before the actual event one week from today.

****

After his first day of work Traveler had probably never
been ridden more slowly as Norman made his way back to
the Belle, as he called the boat. Tired was not the whole
story. His bike went in the storage locker up front and then
he pushed himself up the stairs to the apartment. After a
quick shower he stretched out on the bed and was asleep in a
moment. What woke him about an hour later was something
stroking his hair. What was it? When he opened an eye, there
was Ricky next to him. She smiled and kissed him on his
cheek. "Just checking on you. How did it go? I brought you
something to eat in case you didn't have dinner."

After he got his bearings and sat up, she asked if he liked
eating in bed. He did, but he'd never done it with a woman
before – just a few times when he couldn't stand talking with
his mother at the dinner table and took his plate and went
to his room. "I brought some fried chicken, potato salad and
chocolate cream pie. We can go to the table in the other room
or have a picnic here – on your bed. Tell me which you want
while I get us a couple of beers from the other room."

Between bites Norman managed to say, "Ricky. You are
fun, lots of fun," and did he dare add, "on a bed." He did
say it and her response with a smile was, "Thanks. So after
we eat, do you want to have some other kind of fun? I have
some ideas."

Norman was quiet for a while eating his dinner. Then,
"Honestly. This isn't like me." He hesitated. "I am pretty

sure sex with you will be unbelievable – like I have only fantasized – and waiting is something I'm not very good at." Was he saying the right things? "But I think I need to rest. I have another long workday tomorrow. But, it's my birthday – tomorrow. Can we get together again then? After work? I'll try not to be so tired."

She smiled again. "Forget your bike. As I said, I have some ideas. One is to drive you out to the Speedway in the morning and the pick you up after work so you have more energy. When we get together should I bring food so we can celebrate here?"

****

That evening was more than Norman's greatest dreams about sex. Up to this point fantasies were his total experience, except for hundreds and hundreds of episodes pleasuring himself. Should he tell Ricky his inexperience or did she already know from his halting performance so far? He couldn't tell her.

Her birthday dinner for Norman was topped off with two chocolate cupcakes with white frosting and each with a candle. She said, "Why don't we take these into the bedroom? Maybe we can eat them in bed. Remember how much fun it was last time?"

He was out of his clothes and under the sheet in no time while Ricky went to the bathroom. She came out wearing a filmy cover that clearly showed her breasts and the rest of her toned body. Ricky dropped the cover as she came over to the bed. She sat on the edge and said, "Why don't you get up so I can give you your birthday treat?"

This was all new to Norman. He was nervous and very excited as he stood before her. He was amazed. His erection was right before her eyes. Without hesitating and with desire she said, "My, you are lovely – and I mean all of you all over." Norman was beside himself with excitement. He hoped she didn't see his slight shaking. It got more so when she took her finger and scooped off a touch of frosting from one of the cupcakes and put it on his end. She let it sit there for a moment and said, "I would rather taste the frosting from you than the cupcake." And with that she took him into her mouth.

What flashed through his mind were scenes where women gave men oral sex in the porn magazines that he and his friends passed around, but he quickly pushed those thoughts out of his mind, because right here it was actually happening, but in a tender, affectionate way. His legs started to feel weak. He started seriously shaking and much as he wanted – really desperately wanted – he could not control himself. Then came the explosion. He didn't know what Ricky would do. She looked up at him with her great smile. "Don't worry about this. You wouldn't be a man if you hadn't reacted as you did. After I wash, let's crawl into bed and maybe – later – we can make love." What more could he ask from this woman?

She helped cover him as he stretched out. The kiss she gave him was the tenderest he could remember from Ricky. Long and sweet. He managed to get out from his pillow, "You are amazing. Meeting you was one of the best things that ever happened to me."

"I feel the same way. What I really like about you is you respect me," she said in response and got into the bed. Soon they were asleep in the comfort of each other's arms.

****

Out at the Speedway the next day Norman was a firestorm of activity. Gus said, "Heck the way you're going at it today, we don't need the other workers. What's with you? Oh, by the way, we'll need to leave the stage and all after our afternoon rehearsal since Amy and the others want to do their rehearsal. We can take it down after that. But we'll be plenty busy with another project. See those 14 racecars on the infield? We need to move them around. Again, why are you so happy? "

"Happy to have a job – and I met a woman. What could be better?"

****

The day of the performance, precisely one hour after the last race, the concert announcer got things underway when he said, "Ladies and gentlemen, please look to your left." With that the 14 racecars on the infield came roaring to life and zoomed onto the track to the left of the stage. After some jockeying they began what seemed like a disorganized formation. But quickly two cars positioned themselves into one slanted line and two more cars did the same for the other leg. Now a smaller car tucked itself mid-way between the legs to form a perfect, colorful A. Six of the other idling cars started to move, but it seemed like they didn't know what they were doing. Before most people in the stands could figure it out, those cars had formed into a giant M. Some in the crowd now began to see what was happening and the roar began building. Finally the remaining three cars zipped into a Y. It was deafening. But it got even louder when out of one of the cars at the top of the A jumped Amy, microphone in hand. As she made her way to the stage, she sang a number she had written especially for this performance called "Wheelin". The stands had erupted at this point and her voice was almost overpowered.

When it was over, Norman looked for Ricky to come

across the track to where Gus, he and several other workers were in the scrims set up as the back stage. Rudy was there too. "What did you think of Amy's entrance – with the cars? It seemed to really excite the crowd. I have some other ideas for her entrance in the other cities on the tour," Rudy said.

Norman wasn't really paying attention to what anyone was saying. He didn't see Ricky at first, but then he spotted her athletic walk coming toward him. She looked wonderful. "So what did you think?"

"You guys really pulled off a treat. It was great in every way. Who came up with the idea for the cars at the beginning? I agree with the crowd who loved it. You really should do it tomorrow night too. All this work and all that talent for one performance is not enough," Ricky said.

After a while she pulled Norman aside. "What I really want are several shows like this one to keep you here longer – for as long as possible. It's very hard for me to think you'll be going on the road in about two weeks. That's going to be really difficult for me."

"I feel the same way too," he said.

****

The two weeks before departure for Columbus was bliss for Norman. After that first concert at the Speedway his schedule allowed him more non-work time, most of which he spent with Ricky. He thought she was enjoying the time too because she smiled constantly – and did things that said she was happy.

One of those things was to buy a bicycle. He was surprised one day when he came back to the boat about four o'clock in the afternoon and went to put Traveler in the forward locker like he always did. In the semi-darkness he could see a shiny yellow Schwinn. It wasn't a Traveler, but a Schwinn Collegiate. Then it dawned on him that she had bought the bike so maybe they could ride together.

That they did. One day Ricky suggested they ride to the Japanese Garden at Maymount, a place she had always wanted to visit. Norman and gardens rarely mixed and he was reluctant to go. But the compromise was that he would go with her to the gardens if she would go with him to the Edgar Allan Poe Museum. Afterwards they both admitted to having a good time at the other's choice – she with the ghoulishness of the Poe Museum and he with the vast collection of antique carriages in the mansion at the Gardens.

There was no hesitation when she signed them up for an annual bicycle event in Richmond called the Anthem Moonlight Ride. For that ride they joined 2,000 other crazies dressed up in absurd costumes and lights. Ricky went as a riverboat captain and he as a racecar driver. What else? When they got back to the apartment about two in the morning, they laughed and began to make love in their outfits. The session started out that way, but soon there were hats and jackets and boots being flung around the bedroom and their lovemaking then settled into the tender, sustained pleasure they both had learned to give each other. It was bliss.

But the time for parting came only too quickly. The next morning she asked through soft tears, "How will I know where you are and what you're doing?"

"I'll call. I'm not good at letter writing."

"Can I visit you on the tour?"

"Sure. This month the tour goes to Columbus, as you know, then in July I'll be in Tallahassee; after that Algiers near New Orleans in August and we end up in Laredo in Texas in September. Why don't we work it out to meet in Tallahassee?

"That would be perfect – if I can wait that long."

"But how will you run the boat when you're away?"

"Eric can handle it."

Columbus *July 1984*

A horrible incident

They were both outside the apartment on the top deck of Ricky's riverboat when the blue truck pulled up as planned. It was eight o'clock in the morning and Norman was sleepy from their incessant lovemaking. They both approached the night like it wouldn't happen again. Gus honked and Norman said to Ricky, "I can't just leave you up here, C'mon down and say goodbye to Gus too."

Out on Interstate 85 it was pretty quiet in the truck cabin for the first hour. Gus was driving their equipment truck slow enough that cars, trucks, buses, and RVs – everything else on the road – passed them. Norman seemed not to even notice anything along the way and instead sat in silence even as Gus tried to start several conversations.

"You look gloomy, my friend. What's going on?" No response. So he tried a different approach. "The plan is to stop at a truck stop for lunch in about two hours. Then we'll go to Raleigh to spend the night. Here's the itinerary." Gus wasn't sure he could endure another two hours of Norman's silence, so after a while he tried still another conversation. "You sure like that bike. I was never a bike guy myself. I made sure your bike got onboard, but it's in the other truck."

"Hey, thanks." That was all.

Norman looked over the itinerary without saying anything. He did take note as other parts of the Ramparts entourage passed them on their left. First another equipment truck like theirs pulled alongside and waved and then two luxury motor coaches went by with darkened windows to keep out prying eyes. One was for the staff and another was for Amy. Gus said, "Can you imagine? She gets to ride in luxury – all by herself – while we bounce around in the cab of a truck. Life ain't fair. Actually, she isn't all by herself in that big machine. You may remember her helper Naomi – Amy's constant companion – she's there too."

You couldn't miss Amy's bus. There were three huge letters painted on the side that spelled A-M-Y. To Norman her bus looked more highly polished than the other one loaded with the staff.

"Did you see that car at the front of the procession?" Gus asked. "That's Rudy. He gets to ride in luxury too, but he doesn't have a driver like Amy. But you know what? She is a very talented lady and without Amy none of us would have a job – or at least a job like this. And you saw how many different outfits she wears during the show. Those are all in her bus with Naomi who also does her make-up. Fair warning – just don't ever approach that bus without checking with Naomi first."

Norman was feeling a bit better and so he asked, "You're married, right? Can I ask? How did you know you were in love? I just don't understand love and how it works."

"So that's why you've been so glum all this time." It was Gus' turn to be silent and he was for several minutes. "That question – how did I know I was in love? And your other question 'how it works.' I wish I could give you a simple answer. I have no idea 'how it works.' I do know this – for goodness sake, don't ever ask a woman that question."

More silence. "Yes. I am married – happily I might add. I've learned a lot of things along the way. Hope I have anyway." He reached for his wallet and managed to pull out a worn piece of paper. "Here's something to think about." He handed it to Norman who read, "Young love is a flame; very pretty, often very hot and fierce, but still only light and flickering. The love of the older and disciplined heart is deep burning. Unquenchable." Norman looked up at Gus and Gus responded, "That's me and my wife. I keep that in my wallet to remind me of how lucky I am – and to read to my daughter – the high schooler – probably a little younger than you – because she has already had a couple of broken hearts."

Gus could tell Norman was taking this in and trying to figure out what it all meant. "Advice about love is hard, no matter who is giving it. But maybe that's the good part. It is a mystery. If we knew everything about love, I'm not sure it would be love. Along that line here's some advice – anyway. Don't try too hard to figure it out. That can take the fun out of it. Just enjoy. Let the flame burn. As they say, 'love begins with a smile, grows with a kiss and can end with a teardrop.'"

Actually, Gus enjoyed being Norman's counselor in matters of the heart. That was until Norman said, "You've met Ricky a couple of times – at the first concert in Richmond and again this morning. What do you think?"

"Very pretty. Very athletic-looking. Very nice lady."

"Thanks. You said 'lady.' What do you mean by that?" This was very important to Norman and so he pressed Gus, "How old do you think she is?"

At this point Gus had to maneuver around a slow moving multi-wheel hauler with a bulldozer on its back. He was happy for the interruption because that gave him some time, so he didn't have to answer Norman right away.

He seemed to be ruminating on Norman's question. Then he said, "A woman's age is always hard to tell. I have a hard time with age. I'd say she is a bit older than you – maybe between 25 and 30. But that's okay."

"That's what I thought too – about 30. God, she is so neat though. We've had a great time doing things. Do you think the age difference is a problem?"

"Norman. You keep asking me questions that have no real answers. I'd say if you really enjoy each other, forget about age. I can tell from how you looked when we left that you're going to miss her. That she's really special. Am I right?"

"I'm hoping she can meet me somewhere on the tour – soon. Maybe Tallahassee."

The truck radio was tuned to a pop music station. Norman hummed the words to Captain and Tennille's "Do That to Me One More Time."

"Once is never enough with a man like you…Kiss me like you just did, oh baby do that to me one more time…Do it again, one more time…"

Gus said, "That song seems to fit your situation with Ricky perfectly. I see no reason you two can't be together in Tallahassee."

****

At the truck stop, the vehicles in their entourage were lined up side-by-side with Amy's bus on the outside. That was for promotional reasons. And Norman soon learned why. The truck stop wasn't overly crowded, but when the people there realized Amy – the adored country singer Amy – was right before their eyes, they flocked to her bus. Within minutes there were about 30 people clustered around the door of Amy's bus chanting for her to come out. The noise grew and went on for about ten minutes, when all of a sudden the bus door opened and Naomi stepped out. "Thank you folks. My name is Naomi and I am Amy's assistant. You are very kind to ask to visit with Amy. Travel like we are doing for the tour can be very tiring and Amy must rest between concerts stops. I have spoken with her about making an appearance with you today and she has agreed to come out for a short period of time. Please give me a few minutes to go back into the bus and make arrangements for Amy to appear shortly.

The crowd cheered. And they waited, and waited. About 20 minutes later the door opened and Naomi came out a second time, this time in what Norman considered a pretty exciting outfit – low cut top and tights that showed every curve. He had not seen her like that before. "Thank you, thank you. Again. Amy says it's wonderful to see so many of you in a place like this. We didn't expect such a nice reception here. I wish we could do a concert right now, but you may know we are on the road to do concerts at Fort Benning in Georgia, then Tallahassee, Florida, on to a place near New Orleans and then we wrap it up in Laredo, Texas." Someone in the crowd yelled, "Where's Amy? We want Amy." Then the rest of those gathered around started yelling the same thing so that whatever else Naomi said – "Hope you can make a concert" – was lost in the commotion.

Just then Naomi moved aside and out stepped Amy, dressed in tight jeans, cowboy shirt, boots and hat – all in gold. In the afternoon sunlight she made quite an impression. The crowd cheered loud and long. Then Amy said, "Thank you. It's nice to have fans at our concerts, but we really like fans along the road. We don't have much time here, but if you'll behave, I'd be happy to sign some autographs. Let's start the line with this lady right here."

****

Rudy had found a motel with a big parking lot in Raleigh where the tour could park all its vehicles. For the night Amy's bus was sheltered on each side by an equipment truck so that a curious passerby couldn't see her name. A good part of the need to shield the bus was because they didn't want anything to happen to it. It worked because no people gathered as they had at the truck stop. But that would change in daylight hours, because when they got to Columbus the plan was to drive her bus all through town and the surrounding area to build up interest before the concert.

Norman couldn't wait to get to his room because he had one thing on his mind. He had to call Ricky. He was excited and so when she answered he blurted out, "I miss you so much – already. Please come down here – now." They had not been apart a full day. As the conversation went on Norman, by turns, sounded elated, then wounded, then restrained and then those emotions repeated themselves.

She calmly asked, "How was the trip?" He related the Amy appearance when they stopped once. He didn't have the nerve to tell her about his discussion about love with Gus or his thoughts about her. He was much more interested in saying, "I'm not sure I can wait to see you. Can you come down to Tallahassee? I need to see you." In the end they agreed she would come down to Tallahassee for a short visit. That made Norman very happy.

After the call with Ricky, Norman needed to work off some energy, so he got the key from Gus for the other truck and retrieved Traveler. From the first pedal stroke he was really pushing it. Norman was surprised at how good it felt to ride Traveler—hard. Most of time he didn't know where he was going which also felt good. Raleigh was a pretty big city, but Norman had learned about it wandering around on a bike. Look what it had brought him in Richmond – many things he had never had before like his independence, a job, and yes, a wonderful woman. After a while a thought snuck into Norman's head that slowed him down a little. It seemed like a long time since he had talked with his mother in Richmond without revealing where he was. He guessed he should call her again, since a lot had changed since Richmond. He rode for almost two hours and when he returned to his room he was exhausted. He felt good.

He picked up the phone and asked the front desk to connect him to his mother's number. She answered after two rings.

"Hi Mom. It's Norman."

"My darling. I'm so, so happy to hear from you. I miss you so much. And I love you so much. I know I'm repeating myself already, but I have to say again that you just can't imagine how much I have missed you. This apartment is lonely without you. How are you?"

"I am fine."

"Where are you and are you safe? Has anything bad happened since we talked before?"

"A lot has happened since I called you from Richmond."

"Tell me."

And he did. It sort of flowed out – about his job – about how much had changed since he left home. He did not tell her about Ricky, because he didn't quite know how.

"Congratulations, by the way, on turning 18." She asked, "Did you have a party? Cake and all?"

Norman hesitated just a few seconds, "Ah, yes. We celebrated. No cake though. We had cupcakes instead." He could feel himself flush slightly as a remembered Ricky and the frosting on his bed. If she only knew.

"Well, Mom. Gotta go. Need to get to work."

"Thank you for calling, my darling. Please, please keep in touch."

"I will."

****

On the next leg of the trip, Gus stepped it up and the time to Columbus went by quickly. Norman was lost in his thoughts again, but this time when he opened up it was more to explore the idea of an 18 year old dating a supposed 30 year old. "As I said before, we have fun together. I am really happy with this woman. She seems to feel the same way. She even bought a bike so we could ride together. That tells me a lot."

"That's nice, but a true relationship has to have a lot of pieces to be whole – not just things, but experiences together will make it last."

"I know. Let's say she is 30. That's twelve years between us. Do you think she might get tired of me? That really worries me. She has a lot more experience than I do."

Gus was thinking of how to ask Norman what seemed to him like an important question. Here was a mature, attractive woman, so why with those attributes was she still single? He didn't want to get too deep into this discussion because he could tell Norman was falling for Ricky. But he did have that question. "Do you know if she was married before?"

"She told me she was divorced two years ago. Hasn't dated since. We didn't talk too much about it. What she said was she was in a marathon-training group several years ago and this guy was the coach. He kept offering to train her one-on-one. They got to know each other pretty well and ended up getting married. Big problem. I guess he was abusive, which she didn't find out until later. I didn't ask what she meant by abusive, but it must have been pretty bad."

"That's not good. To me that's reason enough not to want to date. She seems like a mature person. I am sure she wouldn't hang out with you just because you're young.

For her, there has to be something – perhaps a lot – there too. Out on the road like we are, you have too much time to think about her. Remember what I said last time – over-thinking a relationship, like you are, doesn't do much but make you anxious. And besides, we have a lot of work to do on this tour. It's only just begun."

With that, Gus' walkie-talkie came on and it was Rudy telling them, as the itinerary said, to pull into the next truck stop for lunch.

****

At dinner in Columbus all the crew was having a good time. Even Amy appeared in an outfit covered in rhinestones. The person next to Norman said, "That woman is always 'on.' In all the years I've been with this company, I've never seen her in regular clothes. But then again, she's what makes all this possible. But it seems none of us ever gets to really know what Amy is like. For such a public person she seems very private."

After dinner, Rudy called everyone on the tour – except Amy – together to review the concert preparations. "Gus. You and your equipment guys need to take the trucks down to the venue where we'll hold the concert. It's called the Pine Hollow Amphitheater. It's right outside Fort Benning. I believe you have the map. You and your technical people will have to survey the area because we are working with the Army to run cables from the base to the amphitheater. Apparently there isn't enough juice in the amphitheater to run all our lights and sound equipment, so the military will provide us with the extra power. In exchange for that and some additional assistance they are providing – I'll talk about that in a minute – we are allowing them to film the concert to be shown to the troops overseas. They are making all the arrangements for that part of the program. The only thing we have to do is make sure there are electrical cables available on either side of the stage so the video company the Army has contracted with can have power to their cameras.

"Gus, your contacts at the amphitheater and at the Army will be there at ten o'clock tomorrow morning. They are Todd Atkins and Billy Field. I have a session with a Colonel to get background info, but those are your direct contacts. Here are their phone numbers."

Naomi had a question. "Can the backstage area be made much bigger? In Richmond, there wasn't really enough room for all of Amy's costumes and we had trouble making all the wardrobe changes she makes during the show." Rudy gladly had that taken care of since the 25 or so costume changes Amy made during the performance was one of the unique parts of the show.

Then he said, "And now for the show stopper. Remember how in Richmond we had racecars in the infield as though they were there at random? Then they eventually formed into the words A-M-Y and she jumped out of one of the cars. Remember how the crowd loved it? Well, we have something – not similar – but still pretty spectacular for this performance. As background, remember this is Fort Benning and one of the big, big programs here is the jump school for the Army Rangers. Does that suggest anything to you guys? Well, we have arranged with the Army for three jumpers to sky dive before the concert starts – while it is still somewhat light. There will be a red shoot, a blue shoot and a white shoot and the jumpers will be in flowing red, white and blue shiny suits." He was getting excited himself. "Here's the exciting part of the jump – and the hard part to pull off – one of the sky divers will hold a gigantic American flag as he is coming down and as they land beside the amphitheater, hopefully hidden behind the flag, a golf cart will zoom out and deliver Amy, who will be in a similar flowing outfit to the sky divers. If it works, it will look as though she was one of the jumpers. This will take some practice as you can imagine. How does that sound?"

After the group settled down, Gus said, "But that's not all. The concert is expected to end at around ten o'clock and to top it off, we've planned with the Army another jump – but this time it will be a night jump. Again, three sky divers, but this time they will have red, white and blue strobe lights attached to their bodies so that when the crowd looks up, all they will see are blinking lights coming toward them as the divers aim for their landing spot beside the amphitheater. I really believe this is something that will be talked about for years – and it should help us promote the concerts. Oh and by the way – I just heard this concert is nearly sold out. Just so you know, the Pine Hollow Amphitheater has 5,000 reserved regular seats in front. But then there is a sloping lawn above those seats where people can set up their own chairs, have a picnic ahead of time and just relax before the show. We've sold almost 10,000 of those places."

****

Janell had two mint juleps in hand as she made her way over to where Matt was stretched out on a chaise lounge. He was on his stomach and she could see he had been in the pool to cool off while she went for the drinks. She sat down on a chaise next to his and said, "Hi handsome. Oh, that's right. I'm just the cocktail waitress and I'm not supposed to fraternize with the guests. So where's my tip?"

Matt reached up behind himself and accepted his drink without saying anything. After a sip he turned and said, "Hey. You look pretty good. Pretty sexy. What are you doing later? Maybe we could have some fun."

They laughed and when they both went in the pool later, he pulled her over. "What do you think of my resort? Pretty nice, huh?" While he was working with the Trauma Center at 14th Combat Support Hospital at Fort Benning, the Army had arranged for Matt and Janell to stay at the posh Army Lodge on base. It was usually reserved for visiting senior military officers. Like a resort, it had a sizable pool, tennis courts, several restaurants and a small Army museum attached. She said, "Honestly, doctor. I've stayed at some resorts, but this one is great. Pay attention because I may get used to this kind of accommodations. At Walter Reed when we were there last week, the housing was the pits compared to this. How long are we here? Another week?"

A few more laps of the pool and when they were back in the sun on their chaises Matt said, "I may have something for you. When I was at the hospital today, one of the other ER docs mentioned there is a big Amy concert just outside the base a few nights from now. I've always liked her music. Should I get us a couple of tickets?"

Janell had a way of telegraphing her thoughts before she spoke, and from what he could see – just then – Amy was probably not high on her list of music celebrities. She said, "That's – very nice of you, but I'm not really a fan of country music. When you listen at home it doesn't bother me, but country is not something I would seek out. I know you like it. I have an idea. Why don't you get a ticket and go?"

"Maybe," he shrugged. "But I don't think I would go without you."

****

Three days before the concert Rudy was to meet Colonel Tom Barstow at the main Fort Benning gate so he could give him a personal tour of parts of the base. At the guardhouse

Rudy was told to park his car to the right and Col. Barstow would be along shortly. It didn't take long before a dark green sedan pulled up beside Rudy. He immediately noticed the front license plate was a stylized silver eagle, signifying his tour guide's rank. The windows were very dark. A driver got out and opened the door for the Colonel. He came over to Rudy, introduced himself and said he had arranged for a driver today so they could talk more easily. Rudy had no experience in riding with a colonel – with a driver, no less. He liked it.

Rudy's first impression of the base was its spaciousness. Wide open spaces dotted with forests of pine everywhere. And he said so.

The Colonel responded, "That's right. This is a pretty big base. Probably one of the military's biggest in the U.S. It may surprise you that Fort Benning is a little over 200,000 acres and what's remarkable is it serves almost 120,000 people, made up of active military personnel, their families, reserves, retirees and some civilians. This is mainly a training base – known as a Power Projection Platform – starting with raw recruits and moving on up to the intensive and sophisticated Rangers program. Speaking of the Rangers, you can see over there are what we call the Jump Towers. They're pretty tall – about 250 feet in the air. For the training we actually start them on the ground, then move on to the Jump Towers as they gain proficiency and then we take them up in the airplanes. It's one of the most rigorous training programs in the Army. But when they're done, they are very, very good."

"I'm very interested in that program since the Army has agreed to provide our concert with two jumps – before and after," Rudy said.

"That's correct. I actually started the negotiations for those jumps with a man by the name of Robbie at your office in Richmond. I believe he's the big boss. We're happy to provide a couple of jumps in exchange for being able to video Amy's concert. Our plan is to show it overseas through our Army network."

They rode for a while through rolling hills, pine trees and clusters of building. At one point their driver slowed to a crawl as they came across some walkers straggling up the hills with backpacks and rifles. It seemed to Rudy that some of those people looked almost like ghosts – they were hollow-cheeked, hunched over and barely moving forward.

The Colonel said, "Because it's so big, Fort Benning is actually divided into 'communities.' This is Sand Hill. If you're wondering who those people are on the road, they are participants in what's called "The Best Ranger Competition". It is a real test of stamina and training. One of the events is a 30-mile road march and seeing the walkers we just did, you can imagine even that event weeds out some of the entrants. The toughest of all is a section of the competition called Orienteering. It is so called because it is basically land navigation at night. Participants are required to find points they plotted on a map across miles of difficult terrain beforehand, but in the darkness they are not allowed any flashlights or other illumination. If the moon is out it goes pretty well, but sometimes we have to go in and rescue a few of them who get totally lost. Some guys are very good at the whole competition, while others struggle. It tells us a lot about how tough our Rangers can be in tough situations. Although the competition's not mandatory most guys do it as a matter of pride."

Rudy took all this in. For a very short moment he imagined himself in such an event. He just shook his head. No way.

"This is a pretty competitive place. As you can see, the Ranger Competition is going on right now. In the fall we also have an annual event called the International Sniper Competition."

Rudy asked, "Is that what I think it is?"

The Colonel replied that there are up to 30 two-person teams entered each year. "This is the tenth year for the competition and last year we had seven foreign teams. What makes it very challenging is there are 14 events during the competition over 72 hours – six of them are at night. It virtually goes non-stop but yes, they get a break after 24 hours. The whole event tests sniper teams' abilities to engage targets while under the most stressful situations. Like stalking the enemy in urban settings. Last year I overheard one of the participants say, 'It's the best job in the Army to be called a Sniper. I wouldn't trade it for anything in the world.'"

Rudy should have been impressed, but he wasn't because it seemed to him to be a celebration of killing. He said nothing. He needed the Army.

Soon they were at a large power station. The Colonel explained that this is where the electricity for the concert would come from. They met with Todd Atkins to finalize any details.

Before they parted at the main gate, the Colonel said, "There's one other person you should try to meet with. Pete Jorgen is the civilian television specialist the Army has hired to videotape the concert. I believe he's planning three cameras. They are pros, but it wouldn't hurt for your people to make contact with him to coordinate any last minute details. Here's his phone number."

****

The afternoon before the performance was filled with last minute arrangements and decisions. The sound system needed better balance; the expanded backstage area for

Amy's wardrobe had pushed the light hangers too far back and they had to be adjusted; Amy's warm-up band Wave had their instruments in the wrong places. It seemed to Rudy as though this was always the case. He did have one nagging problem. He had phoned Pete Jorgen three times without reaching him and this bothered Rudy. Gus had tried him too without success. His company, TV Systems Georgia, had brought in two tower cranes and set them off to the side of the reserved seating. When he inquired, one of the camera guys explained that while the cranes were in their compact position now, they could be extended almost 40 feet – if necessary to provide better angles – and they would be shooting from both sides of the audience and from the tiny broadcast booth nearly hidden in the sloping lawn. He also pointed out a mixer truck that was off to one side where the producer could switch from one camera to another. That eased some of Rudy's apprehension, but he still would like to speak with Pete. "He should be here soon," the cameraman reported.

****

At twilight the lights dimmed to a spotlight on the announcer who said, "Ladies and gentlemen, may I call your attention to the sky above."

Not that most people in the audience hadn't seen sky divers before since they lived with them daily at the Fort Benning Ranger School, but there was still a feeling of pride as the divers came down with their red, white and blue shoots, highly visible long before their landing. Rudy noticed how the skydivers worked their steering toggles so they made their way down to earth with consummate skill. Beautiful, precision landings for all of them. The skydiver with the giant American flag did his part.

A huge round of applause went up suddenly in response – bursting through the flag in the same flowing patriotic costume as the divers – was Amy, microphone in hand. It worked. The illusion was there perfectly, even for the camera guys who saw the golf cart carry her to the flag and then disappear into the bushes at the side of the stage. They wanted to believe just like the rest.

Among loud cheering and applause, Amy made her way to the stage singing "Fort Benning Blues" with a new set of words from the original. That stirred the crowd even more. They were on their feet. They hardly sat. It was a triumphant beginning.

When Amy was onstage, at the direction of the producer in the mixer truck, the two tower cranes rose to their tallest point to get better shots of the performance and the crowd. In the mixer truck during the performance the producer went from one monitor to the other giving the video different perspectives – side angles, high shots, straight to the stage shots. One of the close-in shots was of a straight-backed military father and his wife with a child asleep in her arms. Another was of a couple, obviously in love, embracing while Amy sang the soulful "So In Love."

"*...Listen, I'm so in love with you, that I can't help myself, can't help it, as long as it's me and you, we don't need nothing else...*" Norman felt she was singing directly to his love for Ricky and her love for him.

At the end of the concert the audience wouldn't let her off the stage. "Encore, encore." After it all finally died down, originally the announcer was to call attention upwards to the sky to end the concert, but Amy was so caught up in the moment that she decided to take that role.

The announcer in the wings was about to make his appearance when Amy subtly waved him off. "And now ladies and gentlemen, we call your attention once again to the sky where we will end this concert as we started it – but this time with a thrilling night jump. Please applaud these brave people who have trained right here at Fort Benning!"

A roar went up as the three skydivers made their way toward earth with red, white and blue strobe lights sparkling in the night. No flag this time, just the lights making a spectacular show, almost like a light shower. Closer and closer they came in unison, just like the first jump –the divers were close to the ground now – maybe 100 feet up. The crowd was at its loudest – whistling, cheering, and clapping – for the just concluded concert and for the skydivers. The noise seemed to grow and grow with their excitement. Then the beauty of it all, the joy, the patriotic feeling of the whole evening abruptly stopped when a strange, eerie crackling sound suddenly blanketed the crowd.

They gasped as they tried to figure out what was going on. No way to sort it out at first as sparks were flying all over the place at stage right. Two of the shoots landed as before, but in the darkness the third diver apparently had hit the top of the television crane that had been raised after the first dive – unseen by the diver in the blackness. There was panic in the audience as the third diver's shoot caught fire, caused by sparks from the TV power line torn from the camera in the confusion.

It was tragic as the diver instantly catapulted forward into the crowd, followed closely by his flaming canopy. Those in his path tried mightily to get out of the way, but that only made it worse. Some were being trampled. Others ducked down between the seats and were free of flying debris, but they still had to fight off hunks of burning cloth. A woman was wailing at the top of her lungs that she couldn't find her child.

It was difficult to tell what was going on in the confusion. Obviously some people had been hurt, to say nothing of the unfortunate skydiver and the television cameraman. Then from the stage came the steady voice of Amy.

"Please everyone, don't panic. Be calm while we get help. Is there a doctor in the house?" While her voice was calm, Amy had a hard time seeing into the lights, which the lighting people left on to help with the rescue operation. Soon the crowd started to yell, "Here's a doctor, here he is," as a man came running forward to the accident scene. He was without any medical supplies, but one of the stagehands was beside the doctor in seconds with the only two First Aid Kits from backstage. "Can you get more of these?" the doctor asked.

"Are there any more doctors, or nurses – or medics here tonight?" Amy asked without being able to see through the lights the four women and a man who had been rushing to assist the doctor. As she looked out Amy could see the crowd disbursing pretty quickly. "Please try to take care as you leave. It looks like we have some medical care on hand, so be careful yourselves." She was handed a note. "Would anyone with a walkie-talkie please rush it to the doctor and nurses at the scene?"

On the ground, the doctor asked one of the nurses to call the on-base hospital to tell them of the accident and to prepare for about a dozen ambulance cases. It could be two dozen.

He knew that would stress the ability of any ER to handle that many cases at once, but until he knew more he had to go with his initial count. Gus immediately handed his walkie-talkie to a nurse who asked the hospital to send as many Emergency Medical Personnel and ambulances as possible.

Now one of the nurses asked for blankets. The best Gus could think of was to send Norman at full speed to both their equipment trucks, parked just behind the stage. The blankets they used for protecting the equipment weren't the best, but they would have to do until the ambulances arrived.

It was at best a stopgap measure, but these blankets allowed the doctor and nurses to carefully move the injured and begin to triage the wounded – to determine medically who needed care the most. The skydiver amazingly was sitting up in one of the seats, but was covered in blood. Several strobe lights still flickered on parts of his body. As a nurse assessed the diver's injuries, Norman gingerly turned off the still flickering lights as best he could and the nurse tended to his head wound. But when she asked how he was, he did not reply. The nurse, not seeing any restriction in his neck, asked if he could feel his palette. That's when she initially determined he had a broken jaw and his palette had been crushed in his fall, which prevented him from speaking. He would need to be taken to the ER among the first to go.

****

They had been asleep for about an hour when the phone rang beside their bed. Janell got up on one arm and as she reached for it noticed the clock said 10:55 pm. "Hello. Yes he's here. I'll put him on." She shook Matt and said, "Honey, it's for you."

"Yes. This is Doctor Hudson." After some silence he said, "That sounds awful. Have you contacted the other ER docs too? We will need everyone, because it sounds like we will be hard pressed to take in that many cases all at one time. We could muster four ER docs, including me, if you can reach the others. Bed space will be a problem. But, yes, I will be there in ten minutes."

Janell asked, "What is going on this late at night?"

Hastily, Matt explained the accident and the need to get to the Fort Benning Hospital ER as fast as possible. He was into his clothes and out the door in five minutes with five minutes to get to the base hospital.

****

In the initial confusion at the accident site, the doctor and nurses tried to bring some order to the situation and in that process handed out assignments to various crew members. Gus over here. Norman to assist one of the nurses over there. What was amazing was that Amy was right there with all the others. She wasn't a bit like the princess he thought she was. Her hair was streaked. Norman now noticed her stage costume for her final number – a leather fringed skirt and jacket with rhinestones – was covered with bloodstains as she moved about to help. Here was their star in the trenches with the rest of them. He was proud for her – and for the rest of their crew, which was helping in any way possible. Norman had time only to reflect on it for a second, and then he was drawn back into the chaos.

He could hear the doctor reporting to the nurses what he found as he moved about the wounded, trying to stabilize them under very difficult circumstances. Some of it he didn't understand from the technical medical terms, but he did decipher such things, "broken leg and ribs, puncture wound to the chest, severe head wound." It was a lot to process. He had never been in the military, but for a moment Norman imagined what he saw here as a possible scene in a battlefield. It was pretty bad. Norman and the others all felt relieved when the doctor told them out loud that he was surprised to see so few burns. He was expecting more because of the flaming canopy, but apparently the fabric had fire retardant. "And that's good because burn victims are hard to treat in an ER, especially when they could have been in big numbers all at once – like here." One of the doctor's biggest concerns was the television cameraman who had not fallen, but had slid down the High-Rise shaft about 40 feet after the sky diver nicked the top of the cherry picker he was in. He did not want anyone touching him, because he feared he had a broken neck and needed the necessary braces before moving him.

One by one the doctor and nurses on site did their best to alleviate the pain and suffering until more hands showed up with more medical equipment and emergency skills. It was only about ten minutes before they heard the sirens. It was a welcome noise as three ambulances rushed to the scene.

The doctor first conferred with the EMTs about the number of victims, which he now counted at 16. As the doctor oversaw the triage, one of the EMTs explained to him, "The problem we have is that with only three ambulances and 16 patients, we'll have to make five trips. We've called for more backup, but we don't know if and when it will show up. What we can use are some of these people to ride with us to assist, not with the medical side, but with helping lift stretchers, open doors and things like that."

Inside the ER, six nurses joined three doctors as they worked to treat all the victims with as much haste as possible. Matt had never been in such a situation before. At his recent visit before this at Walter Reed, outside Washington, it had been almost like being back in medical school. Lots of good banter and good medical emergency discussions. But this would give him a reality check on how this ER functioned under real stress. Tired as he was, he knew he was making a difference.

On their first trip to the base hospital ER Norman, who had been paired with Naomi to help the EMT driver, jumped out and rushed around to the back to help as instructed. Then he and Naomi were back in the front of the ambulance ready to make another run. What he and his uncle Matt didn't know was that at the hospital they were only 50 yards apart and never made contact – not because they didn't want to but because of the tumultuous circumstances – and because neither knew what the other was doing there. It could have been quite a reunion. Both had lots to tell.

****

Over the next several days the question on everyone on the tour's mind was, "What could we have done differently? Could we have helped prevent this tragedy?" Because of the enormity of the accident and the spectacular way it happened, national television and the newspapers came to Columbus to cover it. The media wanted to interview as many of the Ramparts crew as possible, but they were told not to speak to any reporters. Again, Norman was astonished when it was reported by Gus that Amy made an appearance at the hospital to console the victims and she would not allow it to be taped. Here was a woman in the spotlight who lived for such publicity – turning it down. He was proud again.

On Monday Robbie came down from Richmond. They were told they wouldn't hear from him or Rudy until after they had conferred with Colonel Barstow. The colonel had begun an investigation that might take some time, but all the crew was on edge waiting to hear what their two bosses would have to say about the incident. Some had expressed fear of assigning blame and possible lawsuits. While the concert had been a genuine success, it had ended tragically and that weighed on all their minds.

The wait was quicker than expected. There was a message on all their motel room phones that afternoon inviting them to dinner later in a conference room at their motel. Nobody knew exactly what might take place, but nobody would miss the dinner either when they were told Robbie and Rudy would have a message for them all.

"Welcome all of you," Robbie said to get things started after the meal. "First I want to express my heartfelt sorrow for the hurt and pain suffered by the 16 victims of this awful accident. I have some news though – good news – about the injured cameraman with a broken neck. Apparently, the Army medevaced him to a specialty hospital in Atlanta. I have spoken with the ER doctor who treated him here, a Dr. Matt Hudson, and he tells me he is out of intensive care and can use his limbs." There was a collective sigh of relief. That felt good. Amy had tears in her eyes. "Now I would like to call on Colonel Tom Barstow. He has asked to say a few words to you."

Norman didn't pay any attention to Colonel Barstow. Instead he was trying to figure out if the Dr. Hudson just mentioned was his uncle. It had to be. But what in the world was Uncle Matt doing at Fort Benning? How did he miss him? Norman wondered if he could race back to the hospital to try to find his uncle. He was torn. He finally decided leaving at this point could be very awkward, so he turned to listen to the Colonel. And what would he say to his uncle if he did find him?

"My deep thanks are not enough for all you did that fateful night. I would like to individually express my gratitude, but with 30 of you that may not be possible. As we say in the military, 'you stood up.' In our world there is nothing so honorable as doing that. The reports I have received say that time and again 'you stood up' often against all odds in a messy situation. There is one person I will thank personally – and that is Amy. I have been told over and over that she seized the situation immediately and quickly gathered as many medical professionals as she could. It could have been much worse without her quick thinking. And then she tended to the victims like a workhorse." Spontaneously everyone in the crew stood up cheering. The tears now streamed down Amy's face. "One last thing. I don't mean to show disrespect for those who were injured, but we all should be thankful there were no deaths. That is all I have to say. Again – thank you, thank you all."

When Robbie got up again he was silent for a bit and then said. "Coming from the Colonel, that was the highest praise we could have. You make me proud – every one of you. There are a couple of other things I want to quickly cover with you before we all go to the bar. In lengthy meetings with Colonel Barstow, it is clear that this Ramparts crew had nothing to do with causing the accident. It seemed to be entirely on the back of the outside vendor hired by the Army. I know that both Rudy and Gus tried to get ahold of the boss of that outfit before the show, but were unsuccessful. Would that have made a difference? The consensus is it would have. So they may have a problem – and luckily we don't. There is another matter I would like to discuss with you. The subject I want to take up now is the next concert. All of you have been under a lot of stress these last few days. Unusual stress, not the kind we are used to. I have spoken with some of you in person about how we should approach the next concert in Tallahassee and asked the questions, 'Should we postpone it? Should we cancel it? Should we move it to another venue?' Another consideration is that with this delay due to the accident, we won't have as much time as we usually have between concerts. At this point I would like to get your collective thoughts."

There were murmurs as crewmembers discussed it

among themselves. One person adamantly opposed to canceling or moving it was Norman. He and Ricky had set the exact time and place they would meet in Tallahassee and he wasn't about to miss that. But he didn't feel senior enough to express that desire. Instead he whispered to Naomi who was next to him, "Seriously, I think we should go ahead. What do you think we should do?"

Without answering, she stood and said, "For myself, I want to do the concert. I feel it would be good for us. Breaking up the schedule is never a good idea. We need to do that show."

Among all the others, Norman felt Naomi was his best friend among the crewmembers. They had gotten to know each other in the numerous ambulance trips they made after the accident.

And so it went around the room. Not a single person wanted to change the schedule. So it would be off to Tallahassee in a few days. Norman was all smiles. But at this point he needed to race out of the room to see if he could meet up with Uncle Matt. He had to find out if it really was Uncle Matt in the ER the night of the accident. But first he went to Gus to explain why he really needed to go back to the base and could he borrow their truck to get there. In the end he borrowed Rudy's car.

****

As Norman approached the Fort Benning main gate, the uniformed Army guard signaled him to stop. "Where you headed young man?"

Norman pleaded, "I need to get to the base hospital right now."

"Why do you want to go there? Do you have a military ID?"

"No. But my uncle is an ER doc there and I need to see him."

The guard looked over the windshield of Rudy's car for an official sticker. "I'm sorry. Unless you have a military ID and your car has an official sticker, I can't let you on this post. And why would you want to go to the ER? You look pretty healthy to me."

Norman tried to not let his frustration show to the guard, so he asked, "Were you at the Amy concert by any chance?"

"Couldn't make it. On duty. But I heard it was great – except for the accident."

"Well I was there as part of the Amy concert. I was one of the crew taking people to the ER after the accident. And my uncle was one of the docs in the ER, but I couldn't meet up with him. He was pretty busy. So was I. That's what I want to do now."

The guard thought for a moment and said, "In that case, what I can do is call the base hospital to ask if he's there now. What's his name? Pull your car over there while I call."

Norman waited as the guard went into his shack. When he came out he said to Norman, "They told me Dr. Mathew Hudson is not at the hospital now. I asked how to reach him and they wouldn't give me any information. Said it was private. Sorry. To leave, you can make a U-turn around the guard house."

****

After a big buffet dinner, Rudy got up and said, "The terrible incident here has probably gone around the world. Not 'probably.' I know it has because I've heard from lots and lots of people about it. Plenty of you have too. It was hard to turn on a television set in the past several days and not see the accident covered in detail. I'm not sure what effect it will have on our Florida concert, but we need to be aware that the mood may be different and we may have to make some adjustments. What they would be, I have no idea. But you are a creative bunch, so ideas are welcome."

Norman came back into the room at this point to hear Rudy say, "Let me know what you come up with. I propose we get on the road tomorrow so we can have time to work with the university and make this next concert our best so far. Thanks again for being the best crew in the world."

Tallahassee *July 1984*

Big, bigger, biggest

The mood in the truck was quite different on the road to Tallahassee. This time Gus noticed a certain bounciness to Norman compared with his long face as they began the trip to Columbus two weeks ago. He thought it might have something to do with Ricky, so he chose his words carefully. "You seem pretty happy. I know – at least I think I know – that your friend – Ricky – wasn't in Columbus, so what's with you?"

Norman commented that part of his buoyancy was due to the fact it was only a four-hour ride to Tallahassee. "The shorter the better as far as I am concerned. And besides, she's coming down here tomorrow. That makes me very happy. You may not see a lot of me for a few days."

Gus nodded.

****

As can happen in Richmond in the summer, an angry thunder and lightning storm came up suddenly as River Belle was midway in the morning cruise. The accompanying rain was so loud, it made hearing difficult. And the rest

121

of the noise of the storm, mainly the continuous thunder, blasted off the surface of the water which intensified it and scared some passengers into running in different directions. But some passengers – mostly the young ones – fearlessly stuck by the deck railing, some leaning over to catch the sheets of rain in their faces. The crew attempted to direct them away from the apparent peril, but in some cases it wasn't possible to herd all of them away from danger. The result of that storm nearly sunk River Belle.

****

Ricky and her brother Eric sat across the desk from their insurance agent who had come down from Washington, D.C. to investigate the accident. He had some stacks of paper in front of him and didn't say anything for a long time. Then he spread out an array of photos and turned them so Ricky and Eric could see them all. They didn't need reminding of the terrible mess in the river two days ago, but there were the photos – about a dozen of them – showing various angles of the fire that engulfed nearly all the upper deck of River Belle and spread quickly to sections of the decks below. He collected those and then laid out another set. This time the images were of people in the river trying to swim to safety, while one lifeboat floated nearby with no room to rescue more swimmers. You could see fear on the faces of some of those in the water.

"In case you are wondering, the first set of pictures is from the dry dock where your boat now resides. The pictures of the people in the water were taken by someone on shore who saw the whole thing. We have their eyewitness account. Besides the Coast Guard, I am sure the Richmond Police will want to talk with you as well, if they haven't already. We will share our findings with the police and I am sure they will want everything they can get their hands on regarding this accident. Now give me your version of what happened."

Eric started. "First, sir, we want you to know that we have been navigating this river— first with our father and now on our own – for about 20 years. Both of us are fully licensed and go through the Coast Guard yearly inspection. What happened is something none of us expected."

Ricky was next. "My concern is for the people who went in the water and those burned. We've spoken with the EMT and Richmond Hospital people and it is our understanding they are all accounted for and all are mending well. Thank goodness."

"You have radar on board?"

"Yes. Even though our cruises are relatively short in sheltered waters, we have just about every navigation safety device available. Our father was a stickler for safety and he taught us that way," Eric said.

"Again. Please tell me what happened that day."

Ricky thought for a moment. "Both Eric and I were in the wheelhouse. As best we can tell, the lighting struck the radar antenna on the living quarters behind the wheelhouse and that caused the explosion and fire. I know it was the most frightening thing I have ever been through. The lightning struck with such force that it gave off a huge BANG and we couldn't hear anything for a minute or two. It actually jolted the boat with such force that it surged forward and it was hard to keep your balance for a second or two. Before Eric or I could figure out what was going on, the fire broke out on the ceiling of the wheelhouse. It's very old wood and so it caught fire instantly. I grabbed the fire extinguisher in the wheelhouse and it did some good in putting out the fire. We decided Eric would stay at the wheel and try to get the boat to shore as quickly as possible. I went below right away to help with the passenger's safety. The fire spread in patches here and there caused by pieces of the old wooden trim tumbling below."

The man in the suit and tie said, "But why did so many of the people in the water not have on the required lifejackets?"

Eric responded. "It was so sudden. We have seats for every one of our passengers, but lots of people on our tours like to stand by the deck railing to better see the sights along the riverbanks. Before we knew it – when the explosion hit – some who were standing by the railings, we think, were just pitched forward into the water. Others may have jumped out of fear. Immediately, we threw lifejackets to those already in the river. Our crew attempted to give everyone still on the boat a lifejacket. And according to our records from the Coast Guard inspection, we have the required number of lifeboats. But, again, it was so sudden we didn't have time to get them off their chocks and into the water in time."

They all were silent for a few minutes, the insurance person taking notes. Then Ricky said, "To be honest, we felt we were lucky to make it to shore to unload the rest of the passengers. Our immediate fear was that our old wooden boat might sink. Needless to say, that could have been disastrous." Eric nodded his affirmation.

"You say you and the crew made every effort to get the passengers life jackets and life boats. But I have spoken with several of the passengers and three of the injured and they tell a different story." Ricky and Eric looked quizzically at each other. "One injured passenger said there was mass confusion and some panic. And there weren't enough lifejackets for everyone on board. That seems at odds with what you are telling me."

Ricky stiffened and said, "Are you saying we weren't prepared? I know this is just a preliminary inquiry, but the way you are describing the accident makes me very uncomfortable. We firmly believe we did everything we could for all the passengers. If you are trying to set it up that we were at fault so claims can be disallowed, then that changes this whole discussion."

Eric jumped in. "I have to agree with my sister. Look, we are trained professionals – we follow safety rules – our own and the Coast Guard's. This is our livelihood and we aren't about to screw it up. The discussion on your part seems almost accusatory, and if it is, maybe we should get a lawyer."

"I'm only trying to get all the facts. That's my job. As for the legal aspects of this case, that's up to others. But from where I sit, it doesn't look especially good for you. We can't protect you against civil or criminal charges. You know – negligence, dereliction of duty – things like that."

Suddenly Ricky and Eric had a new set of concerns. Apparently those could be huge new concerns. After they left the insurance inspector, they went for coffee to discuss what had just taken place and what to do next. Part of the discussion was whether, based on their just finished conversation with the insurance inspector, they should hire a lawyer. "I don't want to get too worked up because I think we did everything we should have done, but he made it sound like the police might step in any time now. Let's wait on an attorney until we know more, but we need to be prepared," Eric said.

****

When Gus rolled the big equipment truck into the motel parking lot in Tallahassee, it had hardly stopped when Norman was out the door telling Gus over his shoulder that he had to call Ricky right away. "I have to confirm when

I pick her up tomorrow. Can't wait to see her," were his parting words.

Upstairs in his motel room, he dialed her number in a hurry. Why were his hands shaking just a bit?

When she answered, he burst out, "Hi. I can't wait to see you tomorrow. I'm going to borrow Rudy's car to go out there and pick you up. Delta Airlines, right? Oh yes, how are you?"

After a moment Ricky said, "Um. We need to slow down here. I have some news. It's not very good news either." Norman's stomach tightened. What could she be talking about? Was he being dumped? God, he thought that might destroy him.

Tensely he asked, "Dare I ask what this 'news' is?"

She could sense his anxiety and to calm him she said, "You can be assured it has nothing to do with us. I miss you more than I can describe. But I need to tell you upfront, I can't come down tomorrow. I really miss you too and only wish you could have been here to help with the mess we're in."

"Why can't you come down here? What 'mess' are you talking about? You can't imagine how I have looked forward to having you down here – at least for a couple of days. What could possibly stand in our way?"

So Ricky told him about the terrible incident with River Belle. "The real problem is Eric and I don't know what the outcome will be. We've had one meeting with the police and our insurance agent. He didn't make it sound good, but that's an insurance guy for you. We have another meeting with the police and then the Coast Guard. The scary part is if they start accusing us of not having been prepared properly – which is totally untrue – for an accident like we had. There could be liability issues, which I won't go into. We've had a stressful time these last few days and it looks like it may get more stressful. That's why I can't make it now. But enough of that. How are you? You've had some excitement too with everything. I read all about the skydivers in Columbus. That must have been quite an adventure. Do you want to talk about it?" She paused. Norman was silent. Then to lighten things up a bit from all they both had been through, she said with a laugh, "Are we just accident prone?" They both laughed in response and it offered some relief.

He understood why she couldn't make it to Tallahassee tomorrow, but that didn't do much for his deep disappointment in not seeing her. He did talk a little about the skydivers in Columbus, but it wasn't satisfying. The best Norman could do was to get a tentative agreement that Ricky would try hard to make it to Algiers, which was their next concert after Tallahassee. "I'm really upset we can't be together, but Algiers is in two weeks. Maybe I can make it 'til then. I've never been to Algiers, but I'm told it's right across the river from New Orleans. That could be lots of fun." He pounded the bed, which he was glad she couldn't see.

"You know. I have good family friends in New Orleans – actually they were friends of my parents and so they are elderly now. But they are wonderful people. They know the place from end-to-end. That could be fun for us. I'm sure you'll like them"

The best he could think to say to end the conversation was say, "I'd love to see you."

Ricky was hesitant too, but a little more forceful, "I love the word L-O-V-E."

****

Norman thought back on some of the disappointments in his life and decided this was the worst. He sat on his bed for the better part of an hour sorting through all he and Ricky had talked about. God, he missed her. But that wouldn't change what had happened in Richmond.

Then he made up his mind. He wanted the truck key to get out Traveler and ride it long and hard to work out some of his frustrations. So he got up and called Gus who said, "You don't sound the same as in the truck on the way down. What's up?"

"She can't come down."

"You two okay?"

"Yes. Yes. They've had a problem in Richmond with their boat and she has to stay for that."

****

When he got the back of the truck open, he didn't see Traveler at first. He had to move some cables and chairs and tables to find it way back in a dark corner. As he worked to get it out, he noticed two things wrong – a flat front tire and the handlebars had been twisted by whoever carelessly shoved it into the equipment truck. It was no longer in rideable condition. This only added to his frustration.

But he had to take a ride. At this point it was his only solace, so he marched the damaged bike to the motel lobby and asked the front desk person about a good bike shop somewhere close.

"Sure. I ride myself. I see you need some work. There's a shop about three miles from here. You're with the Ramparts group, right? Give me a minute and I'll have our van take you there. Your group has 20 rooms, so this is the least we can do for you. Once you get it fixed, you can ride back."

Now that was some good news. Things were looking up a bit. He asked the desk clerk whether they had any bike route maps. "We don't, but if you want some beautiful rides, you need to get on one of our canopy roads. There are several and I'll bet the bike shop has a map."

While the mechanic worked on his tire and handlebars, Norman asked about bike routes and maps. The mechanic also mentioned the tree tunnel roads or canopy roads. "There are eight of them and together they comprise about 80 miles. They are country roads lined with huge old moss draped oaks – like being in a tunnel. Tallahassee is famous for these roads. Very relaxing." Maybe relaxation was what Norman needed. The mechanic went on, "For more challenging rides we have some great ones too. I'll give you a map, but I really like the Red Bug Trail at Phipps Park. And I often recommend the Magnolia Mountain Bike Trail for some good single tracking. You'll find lots of good riding around here."

Norman didn't plan to, but the canopy roads were so comforting that he did a couple of loops, which he figured was about 35 miles. Once it started to get dark, he pressed to get back to the motel. But he felt much better. Somehow Traveler could help work out some of his kinks better than some of those other substances Robbie – it seemed so long ago – had warned him to stay away from. He was asleep early.

Norman woke up the next morning to an irritating phone call. It was a recorded message from Rudy saying there would be an "all-hands" meeting at eleven to discuss the upcoming concert. Struggling out of bed he said aloud, "That's right. I almost forgot – we have work to do – among all the other things going on."

In the conference room they had set up a projector and screen. A huge logo of Florida State University appeared in the middle. Norman had no idea who the official looking people seated in front were, but he learned very soon that they were from the university. Rudy started off the discussion by introducing first Jim Barnes, FSU's Athletic Director,

Suzie Parsons, the University's Public Relations Director and Clyde Hall, Director of Outreach. Amy was there too.

"These people are here because we are going to take a slightly different approach to this concert. This is not meant to 'spring' anything on you. I had planned to review it with you in Columbus before coming down here, but there were so many other things to deal with, we thought it better to wait – also to see if we would do it all."

The next image that came up on the screen in front was an overhead view of the FSU Stadium.

Rudy continued, "You can see from this diagram that the Doak Campbell Stadium at FSU is huge. Am I right, Jim, in saying it seats about 83,000?" Jim nodded. "All along we planned to use this stadium for our Tallahassee concert. But if we sell 10,000 – maybe 12,000 tickets, that leaves a lot of empty seats. In discussing this situation with Jim and his team at FSU – and with Amy – we have been working on an idea for several months to make this, in a way, a benefit concert. And in light of what happened in Columbus, it even seems more pertinent than ever." Looking to his right he added, "And Amy has been pressing me for some time to do a benefit concert – she says she wants to do something to 'give back.' "

Naomi had a question. "I need to understand. Are you saying, Rudy, that people will pay a surcharge over our ticket price which is pretty high as it is at $100-150?"

"No." And here he turned to the screen. "We plan to have the stage on the field at about the 30 yard line and the expensive seats will spread out from there to the south end zone. We're not exactly sure where the stage will be placed at this point and here's why. The expensive seats will be sold at our usual prices. But you can see all of those could be accommodated on the field without even going into the south end zone. And those people who paid deserve to get the best seats. But that leaves about 25,000 seats from about the ten-yard line all the way to the top of the end zone. Not bad seats at all, but not the premium seats we have sold on the field. Now to give you details on our plan for this concert, I'd like call on Suzie Parsons, the university's public relations expert who you met before."

As usual, Naomi and Norman were sitting together. Under her breath she said, "Don't you think Suzie 'looks' like a PR lady?" Norman's response was, "I've never seen or met a PR lady – but if you say so."

Suzie began, "Folks. It's nice to have you in Tallahassee. We are all excited to host the Amy concert next week. If there's anything we can do to help with the concert set-up or anything you want to know about our town, just let me know. I used to work for the Tallahassee Convention and Visitors Bureau, so I should know my way around. We have what's known as the 'Hidden Tallahassee.' Those are the places and spaces local people go and I would be more than willing to share those with you. They can be lots of fun – and you won't usually see a lot of tourists."

With a slide clicker in hand, Suzie began the pitch. "After the Amy concert was announced about two months ago, one of the bigger non-profits in town came to the university and asked how they could be involved. The Boys and Girls Club wanted to know if they could find a way to become a part of the concert as a fundraiser." Here she took a couple of minutes to tell the group that Boys and Girls Clubs around the country are basically after school programs, mainly for disadvantaged middle school kids whose parents both work. She explained that in the clubhouse they have study periods and then games, sports and events after school to keep kids off the streets and away from temptations like drugs.

"We got in contact with Robbie in Richmond with this idea. The quick answer is that neither of us felt we could favor one program like Boys and Girls Club. Then Rudy and Amy here got involved and as we looked at the stadium, we realized we could accommodate an awful lot of kids – from all kinds of programs like Easter Seals, Special Olympics and Teens-at-Risk – those kinds of kid-oriented nonprofits. Usually for disadvantaged kids. Are you with us so far?" Suzie asked.

There were murmurs as the crew digested this idea.

Suzie then explained that giving or selling much less expensive tickets for non-profits to make money from the concert might hurt Rampart's normal ticket sales and make some of those people unhappy. "But when we checked with your ticket people, they reported the concert was sold out. How many tickets did you sell Rudy?" He responded that one month before the concert, they had sold 12,000 tickets, which was the maximum anyway.

Suzie was excited now. "Being the public relations person I am, we released a story that said in effect, 'The Amy concert is sold out…it's in our huge stadium…what did the community think about Ramparts selling $25 concert tickets that would be bought by local businesses and organizations as a subsidy for disadvantaged kids to come to the concert…and various non-profits would get to keep that money?'"

She reported that the response was huge. Banks, retailers, hotels, and service companies such as dry cleaners stepped forward and before they knew it, another 5,000 tickets at $25 had been purchased. "Look at it this way. Boys and Girls Clubs have 400 members here in Tallahassee and they got businesses to buy that many tickets at $25, which meant they raised $10,000 from your Amy concert. Not bad."

At this point Rudy got up again and added, "Then someone asked, 'What about our military friends down at Pensacola? Can you accommodate those guys too? So soon we were in discussions with the top people at Pensacola and the university and the decision was made to provide – free – 3,000 tickets for the people in uniform, their families and civilian workers at the Naval Station there. So with all that, we will have a pretty good-sized crowd for the concert. Looks like we'll about fill the south end zone. Amy, do you want to add anything?"

She had slipped out of the room and danced back at Rudy's invitation in an FSU cheerleader's uniform. Backed by actual FSU cheerleaders, Amy went through some simple routines. The crew knew a good show from their star, so they stood and cheered as the words were flashed across the screen in front. It was raucous, but lots of fun.

When things had calmed down Amy said, "You know, we've never done anything like this before. It's going to be different and we'll need every one of us to stretch to make it work. I can guess the lighting guys will be challenged, just like the sound people – and all the rest of us. But you guys always come through and we expect this concert to be one of joy and happiness. I think it's a great idea, especially after Columbus."

With the memories of Columbus still fresh in everyone's minds, Rudy hesitated to tell them the Navy had offered to have the Blue Angels, which were stationed at Pensacola, do a fly over of the concert in appreciation for the tickets for their personnel. Nobody else knew of this offer and no final decision had been made at this time, but he knew it would add to the drama of the evening. Who should he discuss it with?

****

In spite of all the fun Norman still felt periods of gloominess. Not having Ricky in Tallahassee was tough for him. He knew there were good reasons why she wasn't there, but somehow that didn't help. At lunch Naomi asked, "Why the long face? As Amy said, 'we're gonna have some fun!' But you? You look sad at times. What's up?"

"I'm heading out on my bike to work things out after lunch. That helps."

"Here's a thought. Amy is away for a couple of days visiting relatives in Orlando. We're planning a little 'dinner' party in our bus this evening. Why don't you drop by after your bike ride? Maybe that will help you to cheer up."

****

Norman followed the bike shop's map and rode with fervor towards Phipps Park and the Red Bug Trail. Traveler wasn't really meant for trail riding, but he put the bike through its paces and was thoroughly satisfied with his performance. He was surprised at how forested the area was with thick trees and underbrush. He stopped once to take it all in, but was back on the trail quickly. He was gone for about two hours of hard riding.

Back at the motel, he showered and was sitting at the desk when he glanced out the window at Amy's bus in the parking lot below. He thought, "That's right. Naomi mentioned a get together. Maybe. For now I think I'll take a nap."

When he awoke, the clock beside his bed said 9:30 p.m. Norman remembered Naomi's bus gathering and didn't spend a lot of time deciding he could use some party time. Was it too late? Probably not. He went to the window in his room and could see – even through the tinted windows – that lights were on in the bus.

When he knocked on the bus door, there was no response at first. After a second time, he could vaguely see Naomi come down the steps to let him in. As soon as she opened the door, he could smell the weed. Some booze too. Not a lot of noise, but a shriek of laughter caught his attention. He hadn't seen Naomi dressed like this since the tour bus stop – in a very low cut top and skintight jeans. He thought she was without a bra. She was beautiful.

"Hi. Glad you could come. C'mon up." She grabbed his hand and pulled him up to the main floor of the bus. It was pretty dark, but he could see the front part of the bus was set up as a snug lounge. It seemed people were crowded all over the place – some on the narrow settee, some in the swivel chairs and even a few on the floor. He could make out about a dozen men and women, some sitting solo and others entwined in a way that reminded him of a sculpture he'd seen in a museum. Booze bottles were spotted here and there and several pizza boxes – mostly empty – were on every surface including the floor. The smell of weed was much stronger now. Still holding his hand Naomi said, "Let me introduce you to these people."

Making her way through the bodies she said, "Hey everyone. This is Norman. He's part of our crew. I invited him because he needs some cheering up." With that a small, thin blonde squinted at Norman, got up unsteadily and came at him. He flinched a bit when she got up on her tiptoes and gave him a big kiss on his mouth. "OK mister. Did that cheer you up? Did you like that? There's more if you want it." Then she slumped down to the floor again and took a hit offered by her companion. Her companion smiled as she began to nod off in his arms like a baby.

Norman had mixed emotions about this scene. He loved parties, but this was different than what he was used to because it was adults. Weed didn't bother him, nor did the liquor. But there was a good deal of flesh apparent – starting with Naomi – and he didn't know quite how to take this lustful scene. Normally he would have tried to make his way into what was going on – to try to get in on the action – but he held back.

Naomi pulled him down so she could whisper in his ear, "The men are from Amy's band Wave. You probably recognize most of them. The girls are groupies they invited along. I know the band member's names but not the girls. We'll make our way through these guys and I can show you the rest of the bus." Just then Barry, who Norman recognized as the Wave guitarist, held up a hand and said loudly, "Stop." Nobody else even noticed. "Young man, you need a hit," and started to hand Norman a half-smoked joint. Naomi intercepted it, took a hit and passed it to Norman. He didn't go deep.

She said, "We'll get you your own in a minute. Would you like a drink? We've got everything." So these were the temptations Robbie warned him about in his office back in Richmond. This was a nice party, but not much different from others he had been to in high school. What's wrong with a little pot, some food and maybe a drink? Then in one of the dark recesses of the lounge he saw two bodies moving rhythmically. It didn't take much imagination to know what was going on. And no, he had never seen anything like that at any of his buddy's school parties. When and if he ever got back to Alexandria, this would add to the many tales to be told to his friends – who seemed a long way off – in another world. He didn't believe any of them had experienced even half the things he had since getting away from hearth and home.

Somewhere Naomi had come up with another joint. They leaned against the wall and this time Norman went deeper. With his first light pull, and with this one, he started to feel that opening up – of the world – way up – that he always felt with weed. He asked Naomi, "Are my eyes slightly buggish? Are we in a fishbowl? I feel like my eyes are like a fish-eye lens. Fishy." Then he made a fish face. He laughed and she laughed. It was hard to stop, but it did suddenly when she pulled him down and gave him a kiss on the lips. He wasn't good at mixed emotions. Thoughts of Ricky flickered through his head, but on the other hand what's wrong with one little kiss? He became slightly confused when she asked, "Where does this go from here?"

He concentrated and then not wanting to seem inexperienced he asked, "Isn't that a question I should ask?" He was pleased with the way that came out.

She grabbed his hand again. "Let me show you the rest of the bus." On the left Norman could make out the closet that held dozens of Amy's costumes as Naomi rolled back one of the doors. It was a blur. She was rambling on about the costumes and how they were made and where they were made and who made them. His mind was not on costumes. It was sorting through what he had seen since he followed Naomi up the steps of the bus. A few feet later and she opened a door to a softly lit bathroom. He had a hard time focusing on the fancy fixtures, the huge array of makeup and the monogrammed towels. "This is my bathroom. Amy's is much fancier. The next door is to my bedroom."

****

Rudy was a producer and his job was to make each show different than the others. When he sat down with Amy to go over the program he said, "You are the star Amy – the draw – but we both know that adding drama wherever possible adds to the overall performance. Because we are providing all those tickets to the Naval Station at Pensacola, they have offered a Blue Angels fly over of the concert. You know how dramatic that can be. But I think it should be at intermission. The Columbus accident was an enormous mess, but it had nothing to do with us – thankfully. And I don't think we should pull back because of that. How about you?

Her only question was the timing. Would the audience be able to see the airplanes, because wasn't the concert at night?

"Remember. We decided to start the concert early because of the kids. Intermission should be at about 7:30, just as the light is going down. That could be even more dramatic. And they'll have on their lights." He could see Amy was okay with that. "Now to the other part I mentioned. An outfit from Orlando heard about the outreach part of the concert. To the kids and all that. They think it's great what you are doing. So they approached me about starting things off with one of their sky writers spelling out A-M-Y in huge letters above the FSU stadium – before the concert starts. I think the kids will love it."

"We certainly are using the sky a lot for these concerts. But I think that's too much. Why don't we stick with just the Blue Angels?"

****

This was the biggest audience Amy and company had ever played to. Lots of energy, especially from all of the kids. Most had never seen anything like a big-time concert and so there was lots of anticipation of what was to come. Finally, the announcer came on stage, welcomed everyone to the very special concert and then said, "It gives me great pleasure to introduce the governor of Florida, the Honorable Phillip Jackson." Some in the audience rolled their eyes. How long would this take? They wanted Amy. They applauded politely.

"I want to add my welcome to all of you. You know, my office is right over there at the state capital – you can see it from some of the higher seats – so I didn't have far to come. But no matter how far, I would have come anyway to deliver a huge 'Thank You' to Amy and the wonderful crew for putting on this show for the many kids in the audience. Many of you might not have been able to see a show like this if it weren't for the generosity of Rudy Feldman, the show's producer, and the star of the show Amy. To you and everyone else involved with this show, please accept my great thanks."

That wasn't bad. The crowd roared for a respectful time.

Then the announcer appeared again. "Thank you, governor. Let the show begin."

Algiers August 1984

Very French

At dinner Norman was initially a bashful participant in one of the rituals of old-money and old-culture Algiers. Ricky had told him some tidbits about her family friends, the Richelieus, beforehand, but he wasn't prepared for the formality of the meal or the different food.

When Bea – Norman assumed she was a servant because of her white frilly apron over a black uniform – came from the kitchen into the dining room, she announced she would be serving the appetizer which was "Vichyssoise de Congrette." As she went around the table first serving Mrs. Richelieu and ending with Norman, Henri Richelieu looked at Norman and said in a kindly way, "She's serving us a cold potato soup with zucchini and leeks. I hope you like it."

Norman had never been exposed to anything like this room, the people, the food, or the servants for that matter. To begin with, Henri wore a suit and tie and the lady of the house, Nora, was in a swirl of a flowered dress with what seemed to Norman to be jewels hanging everywhere. He had taken only a few sips from his wine goblet, when another servant swept in behind him and filled it again. Wine was not his favorite, but now it tasted pretty good. He decided to smile a lot and pretend he wasn't as uncomfortable as he was.

****

Even before they left their hotel room in New Orleans to take the ferry across to Algiers, Ricky had explained to Norman that the dinner they were about to have with the Richelieus would probably be different than what he was used to. "They are an old French family going way back, I believe, to the early 1890s. The couple we'll have dinner with tonight were close friends of my parents and so they are from an earlier era. But I love them dearly. The two couples knew each other because of the boats each family owned – ours on the James and theirs tied up right here in New Orleans. Don't be overwhelmed by the house when we get there. You may have a picture in your mind's eye of what a southern plantation is like. Well, this one will fulfill your imagination. It's pretty big. As I remember it's called 'French Colonial Plantation style' with columns out front."

"On family visits as a kid, I used to go there and pretend I was some damsel in distress and a handsome soldier would come along and rescue me. Eric was always out in the yard pretending to be a plantation boss telling the help what to do. The only real difference with this house and those other big ones out in the country is the amount of land they sit on. The one we are visiting tonight is in town and so the grounds are small compared to The Moors Plantation, which we will visit downriver in a couple of days."

****

Bea announced the next course as "Salude de Tomate Noix et Fromage Bleu." Norman had never heard food described this way and when he did, he took an extra gulp of his wine and nearly choked. Sensing his guest's possible discomfort Henri translated with a smile, "It's tomato salad with blue cheese dressing." Ricky looked over at him and Norman got the message that he should slow down on the vino. Ricky had told him it would be very "French" visiting the Richelieus and as far he as concerned it certainly was that and more.

With just enough wine himself, Henri Richeliu began to regale his guests with stories of Algiers. "This is really called Algiers Point, because if you look at an overhead map you'll see we stick out into the Mississippi directly across from the city of New Orleans. Originally Algiers – or so the story goes – was named by some Frenchman who had been in North Africa before coming to the states. And he liked the name. It was headquarters for the slave trade at one time. Then after the Civil War, Algiers became a major railroad hub. Out east of town there is a vast amount of vacant land that was the old railroad yard. Various ideas have been proposed for that land but nothing has materialized. In spite of all those changes, we still have a small town atmosphere. Although we're only separated by the Mississippi, we're far removed from the hustle and bustle of the French Quarter."

Bea appeared again holding a large silver serving dish. This course, according to her latest announcement, was "Crevettes a la Champingnon." Now Norman had to have another swallow of wine. When she served the main course to him, he was pretty sure it was some kind of shrimp. But now Nora translated. "Norman, I hope you like this course. It is one of my favorites. It's tiger prawns sautéed with wild mushrooms and white wine garlic sauce. Ah, the sauces. That's the secret. It is finished with a parsley and lemon sauce."

Henri asked what they planned on doing while in New Orleans. Ricky was first. "We're going down to The Moors in a couple of days. You know that plantation is one of my favorite places – besides this wonderful house, of course. Norman has work to do, so while he's setting up for the concert, I plan on spending a little time re-visiting the city. I have some business to attend to as well. I believe I told you about the terrible fire we had on River Belle. I have to deal with the fact our insurance company at first wanted to make our lives miserable by saying we were responsible. I think we are over that and I expect they will pay, but I have to stay on top of that one. Thank goodness our boat is in dry dock as we speak. We hope to be back in business in a couple of months."

"I know all about fires in river boats and how devastating they can be. Your situation sounds very familiar. Remember Nora, when our insurance company wanted to shut down our boat, the River Queen, when we had a major fire about ten years ago? At first they said it was our fault and wouldn't pay. It took several months and a lot of our attorney's time to get it straightened out. I'm so glad you have it worked out, Ricky."

Henri said, "Now on to pleasanter subjects. I asked what you had planned for your free time. New Orleans' music is jazz, as I am sure you know. Do you have any interest in going to our place in the French Quarter? We never go ourselves anymore, but you can be sure of hearing some of the city's better music at our club. Any interest?"

Norman was quick to respond that he was very interested.

"Good. I will get you two passes to Le Maison Musique. Ricky, you know for several generations our family has owned the building in the French Quarter where the club is located on Rue Raul. It's upstairs. Very small, but that's because you have to be a member – or guest – to go. It's not for tourists. Norman, if you need passes for any of your people, please let me know how many. The manager's name is Pierre DePaul."

As they finished the Mousse Chocolat Avec Crème Chantilly et des Petit Fruits, Henri said, "We're a bit old-fashioned around here. So I would like to invite Norman into the library where the men can talk. Have you ever had a real Cuban cigar before, Norman? You can have French chicory coffee or brandy with your cigar. Nothing better than a good cigar and a brandy. And the ladies can enjoy tea in the garden in back and talk over things that are important to them. Shall we?"

****

Under a grape arbor with fragrant jasmine heavy on the evening air, Nora and Ricky settled in with tea brought to them by Bea.

"We've only spent a little time together to get to know him, nevertheless I really like your young man, Ricky. He didn't say a lot, so tell me about him."

"I am sure you noticed the difference in or ages. I'm a few years older. It may bother him more than it does me. I'm not sure though. Let me see if I can explain why I find him wonderful. Aside from that disaster with my husband a few years back, the men I have dated since are what I call 'posers.' What I mean by that is they are always trying to impress with what they know, what they do and how they do things with their friends. That gets tiresome after a while, so I haven't dated in some time. Matter of fact it's been a couple of years. Now Norman. He is so refreshing. He is so himself. I've never seen him act out a part. Will that change? Maybe. But for now I enjoy him tremendously. And it is mutual. I like being myself too, which I can completely do around him."

"Do you think he was uncomfortable at dinner tonight?" Nora asked.

"I haven't met his mother, but he tells me she has a big job in DC. Deputy something with the federal education department, so it seems he grew up in a good household. His favorite uncle is a doctor who specializes in emergency medicine. He's an only child and his parents are divorced. But he's never complained about either his mother or father. I don't know a lot other than those few facts, but more comes out each day. I don't want to push.

"To answer your question about dinner. I think your wonderful French food, served by Bea, Uncle Henri's and your musings about this area – they are things he had never experienced before. But I think he handled it well, don't you?"

"Yes, he did certainly handle it all very well. And my, that sandy hair…I shouldn't say this at my age, but I think he's very sexy. Tall and lean. Anyway, if you two are happy together, what could be better? As you well know Henri and I only want the best for you. We consider you a daughter – as though you were one of our own. We loved your parents and I know they would be very proud of you. How is Eric? "

Ricky explained that after their father died, she fretted about how the business would carry on. "Should I have worried? Eric is a pretty good partner. We share duties pretty evenly and so far it's worked out. This recent fire tested our relationship, but I think we're still okay. Even though dad set it up that we're fifty-fifty partners, as the older sibling I still have to take charge at times. I think he resents that – because it's the male/female or maybe the age thing. Here I seem to be talking a lot about age differences again. Must be on my mind."

"What about your daughters – Cici and Baby," Ricky asked.

"They're both fine. Both in New York, doing well, which

makes our visits easy. Cici's designing clothes for one of the big houses and Baby is practicing community law, whatever that means. But Henri's not as fortunate as your dad."

"Why do you say that?"

"Look what you just told me about you and your brother. I sensed from what you said about Eric there could be tension at times, but you manage to carry on and run the business. Neither of our daughters had any interest in Henri's business which has been in the family for two generations. I think it bothers him at times. He has a very competent manager, but I know it will be painful for him to sell it."

****

Norman chose chicory coffee to go with his Cuban cigar. Neither seemed to be as good as promised, but he really enjoyed talking with Henri in his book-lined library. Norman wasn't sure, but he guessed Henri was what – fifty years older? It didn't seem to make any difference.

"Norman. Ricky tells me your group is putting on a grand concert in a week or so– let me see if I can remember what she called it – Amy's Country Music Festival. I think that should be quite a draw, but don't forget this remains jazz country. I still have ears and eyes across the river and one of my old friends told me a couple of things. He said you are planning on using the open area where the railroad yard was here in Algiers for the concert and you hope to stage a surprise entrance for your star on one of our famous Mardi Gras floats. Those will be challenging. But I can help with both. I know the Director of Land and Natural Resources that covers both the New Orleans and Algiers Parishes. If you need anything from him, please let me know. He owes me some favors anyway. As for a parade float, do you know which krewe you are working with?"

Norman had given up on the bitter chicory coffee by now, but between puffs on his cigar he said, "I don't have anything to do with any of our venues except to help set up the stage and lights and sound system. I can check with my boss to see if we need anything for the concert location. But I don't know much about the krewes, as you call them."

"The original floats were built in France in the early 1800s. They were horse drawn and most used the official colors of purple, gold and green. The whole idea of Mardi Gras has grown tremendously over the years to the point that today some people feel it has gotten out of hand. At one time some of the floats had grown – it seemed like – to half a football field long. I heard of one float that held 225 people on board. That's nearly unmanageable given the chaos that can be carnival. Several of the krewes have their 'dens' in Algiers. Those are the warehouses where they store the floats, refurbish them if they need it and make any changes they want.

"For years we had the Riverboat Krewe and our float was a replica of our boat, the River Queen. I always thought it was outstanding with a huge stern wheel turning slowly and throwing off candy and beads, which are traditional at Mardi Gras. But apparently that was too tame for most of our krewe, so over the years they turned it into a pirate riverboat with guns and cannon and swashbuckling pirates hanging off the sides. The crowd loved it, but eventually that got to be too much for me, so I stopped the whole thing. It's quite a ritual, but I don't go near any of it anymore."

Henri paused to finish his brandy. "Tell me if you want to know any places to visit while you're here. I know Ricky mentioned The Moors Plantation. That is a must. As I said, you will get the best jazz in New Orleans at our private club. There's gambling if you want – lots of it. One of my favorite walks is the dike that runs for miles along the Algiers side of the river. As I mentioned this is Algiers Point, sticking out into the river. For many years we had bad flooding until the engineers made it higher than most of the dikes around here to keep the river from making a short cut across our land. Beautiful views of the river from up there. Those are some ideas you can add to Ricky's familiarity with this area."

Soon there was a gentle knock on the library door and Nora entered with Ricky. Knowingly Nora asked, "And what have you men been talking about? I can only guess. I'll bet it's business. Ricky says you have a long day tomorrow and so it must be time to get back across the river to your hotel. I think I can speak for Henri when I say we've had a wonderful time."

****

Norman had his arm tightly around Ricky as they stood on the ferry railing looking across to the lights of the "Big Easy" as New Orleans describes itself. After the ferry pulled away from the dock Norman said, "Sure, Henri and I talked about business. But he also gave me some ideas of what to see and do. So what did you and Nora talk about out in the garden?"

"What if I told you it was mostly about you?"

"That's embarrassing."

"Let's change the subject then," she said with a laugh. "I love this city." They had almost docked on the other side when Ricky said, "I love being with you. And I love you."

When Norman took her in his arms, they could feel the bump as the ferry nudged up against the dock. He caressed her face before he gave her a long, sensuous kiss. "I love you too."

Another long kiss was not interrupted by the sound of several engines starting behind them. They didn't stop either when car lights started flashing on as more engines fired up to leave the ferry. They did stop their kiss, however, when one of the cars hesitated at the top of the off-ramp and a woman rolled down her window.

"You are one lucky girl," she said.

Ricky smiled. "Yes, yes."

****

At breakfast the next morning Ricky said she wanted to go for a run after her phone conference with Eric back in Richmond.

Norman said, "That sounds good." Norman thought for a few moments then said, "I have an idea for both of us. I have to go back over to Algiers this morning to meet Gus. We're going to the den where the chief member of the – I think it's called the 'Absolute Dragon' krewe – is to show us the float we want to use for Amy's grand entrance to the concert. It's some sort of huge fire-breathing dragon where Amy will sit way up on top like the queen. My meeting should be finished around ten o'clock. Last night Henri told me about the dike and berm that runs all along the Mississippi on the Algiers side. It's supposed to be a sight not a lot of people see. High up because of the bend in the river. I can get Traveler out of our equipment truck. Why can't I ride while you run along the pathway on the dike Henri told me about? How does that sound?"

"There's nothing like that along the James River at home. Sounds great." They went for miles stopping now and then to marvel at the sight of the Mississippi moving slowly south. Norman was surprised at the number of tugs and barges and big ships moving up and down the river. It was fascinating – mesmerizing at times. It made the James seem pretty small by comparison. When they got back to the ferry landing, Ricky pointed across the river to the River Queen, Henri's riverboat. She said it looked regal from where they were – all white, prim. Its several layers of lacy trim gave it a lightness in spite of its size. And the stern paddle wheel could be an old-fashioned bustle she said.

****

The next day the one-hour ride to The Moors took them through typical Louisiana countryside – heavy oak trees laden with moss along open fields of tall sugar cane or lower down cotton. Periodically in more forested areas, they could see a long tree-lined drive and catch just a glimpse of a southern plantation house in the distance. And always to the left – not far away – was the Mississippi. This was all new for Norman. He had become accustomed to the James since meeting Ricky. But this was entirely different. And remembering back to Alexandria, the Potomac River seemed like a big lake. Where he and his mother lived there was almost no bustling river traffic like here. Mostly just pleasure boats on weekends.

At The Moors they joined a group after lunch led by a trained docent. She told them, "The Moors was actually built by a sea captain by the name of James Campbell. In 1880 he came up the Mississippi in his ship, the Falls of Clyde, to take on a cargo of sugar and cotton. Even then the port authorities inspected shipments like this and they were going to assess James $50 per ton in port fees. Being a true Scotchman, he refused to pay that amount. After much haggling, along came another ship owner and he bought the whole thing – James' ship, the crew and the cargo. Happy, James took that money and invested it in the 10,000 acres that became The Moors. He built this magnificent home and all the out buildings you will see as we go on the tour – also from the proceeds of the sale of his ship. As a plantation owner, he became fabulously wealthy and at one time his empire reached far beyond The Moors. I am told he eventually amassed land that totaled about 40,000 acres in this part of the world. Any questions?"

A hand went up. "Yes. That is a lot of land. What happened to it?"

"Interesting question. James ran it all for about 40 years. His heirs – he had five daughters – decided after his death that running the whole operation was too much and so over the years they sold most of the land. Now the gardens around The Moors are about 20 acres. Can you imagine going from 40,000 acres to 20? Quite a change. But his daughters did a wonderful thing. They set up a trust for the property that supports maintaining the buildings and the grounds. Then they gave the property to the National Trust for Historic Preservation. So we all benefit from James' astuteness in selling his ship. Any more questions? Okay, then follow me as we tour first the house and then the grounds."

Ricky took Norman aside and said, "Do you really want to see the house? I have something else in mind for you – for us. Interested?" Norman was, of course, intrigued.

As the group headed upstairs, Norman and Ricky quietly peeled off and went outside.

As they passed some of the formal gardens at the back of the house, Ricky took his hand and said, "Consider me your docent from now on." Norman asked what she had in mind. "Follow me."

Soon they made their way down a pathway that was practically invisible from all the other parts of the house and gardens. Ricky obviously knew the way, because after a few yards the trail was almost non-existent. The trees and shrubs had grown onto the path so that in places it was dark. And now the house had disappeared entirely. The only sound was the birds.

Still making their way slowly – suddenly they came to some stone steps that led up to a grassy platform. They walked under an arbor of brilliant colored bougainvillea and when they stopped in the middle, Ricky reached up for a kiss. At the end of it she said, "Isn't this heavenly? I used to come here as a little girl. Even then I thought it was a romantic setting. Welcome to the Secret Garden. I always thought of it as my Secret Garden. That no one else could come here."

Norman kissed her again. Only this time he reached for her lovely breasts. Ricky said, "See that gazebo. Let's go over there."

He took off his shirt and laid it on the bench so they could sit. A huge magnolia tree overhung the gazebo and shielded most of it from view. The aroma was hypnotic. Ricky could hardly resist stroking Norman's bare chest, which stimulated both of them. Norman reached for a white blossom nearby and took one of the petals and lightly brushed it around Ricky's cheeks and neck. Her eyes closed as he did it. He slowly took off her blouse and undid her bra. Now he used the rest of the blossom to softly stroke her breasts. She opened her eyes and with quick motions helped him out of his pants and shorts. His response was immediate. Now it was her turn to gather a blossom, which she used to tenderly wrap around his penis. In seconds she took his erection in her mouth.

Only the birds could see what transpired after that. But if they had had a video camera, what it would relay was love-making of extraordinary tenderness and length.

When they were finished, they sat for a long time just holding each other. She nuzzled under his chin and covered him with kisses. He could not restrain from kissing her neck and down to her breasts. When it all ended, it was late afternoon. The way back to the main house had a certain glow from the sun that shone here and there through the heavy foliage overhead. Now the Secret Garden had special meaning for Norman too. They were so happy.

****

Over the next several days Norman was very busy with preparations for the big concert. Just having Ricky present in New Orleans caused him to work harder than he usually did. He practically put up the stage structure – including the scaffolding for the scrims – by himself. One day Ricky came over from the city while Norman was in the process of hanging the loose material to form the backstage area. He had a big roll under his arm as he started up the ladder. At some point the material started to unroll and much of it got twisted around him and the ladder when a breeze came up. Luckily there was a bunch of the scrim at the foot of the ladder as he lost his balance and pitched into the soft pile of material. Ricky rushed up on the stage and with a worried look on her face started digging Norman out of yards of cloth. Before he emerged, she could hear chuckling. When she thought about it, it was pretty comical. Through the mess he saw her and signaled for her to join him in the pile. She hesitated, but he was enjoying himself and so she practically dove in. He whispered, "Wanna make love right here? There's no one else around right now. Perfect time."

She said in a low voice, "You're kidding, of course. As you know I love to make love with you practically anywhere. But I'm not an exhibitionist. When will you be finished so we can go back to the hotel and have sex – for dinner?"

Norman used the cloth to muffle his response. That was good because he gave a virtual scream, "Yes. Yes." As they were unwinding themselves from the layers of cloth, just then Gus drove up. "Hello love birds. Norman. Looks like you need some help with the scrims. Where is everybody?"

The decision was to wait until tomorrow when all hands would be around to finish the stage. So off went the two lovebirds. Norman had an idea, which they talked about on the way to their hotel. "I like all this French stuff. Very different. But I always thought – I've been told – the French are great lovers. Can we go back to our hotel, pretend we are French and make love like the French?"

"Absolutely," was Ricky's reply.

****

It was expensive, but since this was New Orleans, Rudy was determined to start the concert with Amy's surprise arrival on one of the more elaborate Mardi Gras floats making its way down the main Algiers street and onto the field where the stage was set up. They first looked at the Dragon Float. But it didn't fit any theme they could think of. It took several days, but Rudy and Amy finally settled on a colorful balloon float from the "Air Force Krewe." It was a riot of color. For fun, it was called "Ballooney Toons." It was only a year old which meant many concert attendees probably had not seen it before. And it fit with another airplane idea Rudy had to start the show. Amy suggested her first number could be "Up. Up. And Away. In my beautiful Balloon." When she was onstage and as she started singing, the crewmembers in the float would release thousands and thousands of balloons of every color. The Ramparts crew loved the idea. The only thing that remained to be decided was who would ride in the float with Amy. They needed ten bodies from the crew of 30, so they set up a lottery. Since his work was done, Norman joined in the contest and was one of the winners. He only agreed to participate if Ricky could join them. No problem since many in the Ramparts crew had heard about her, but never met her. Who was this woman Norman was pining for in Tallahassee?

During the inspection Norman noticed that what was interesting about the balloon float was that it had several tiny interior compartments built into the float for storage. Once the eleven people were inside and the float was underway down Algiers Way toward the concert, Norman directed Ricky into one of the small spaces and pulled the curtain. He had a question. "Can we have a 'quicky' on the way to the concert? That would be amazing."

"Hmm. Not enough time," was her answer. "You know how I like to take it slow and easy. It would be fun. Maybe after the concert we can come back here. I never like to miss a chance to make love with you."

****

Rudy, always the showman, had one more treat – besides the float and the huge burst of balloons -- for the crowd as Amy opened the concert. When she began singing an offstage announcer said to the crowd, "Please look skyward to the west."

What the audience could see was a small airplane circling around the area. Up and down it went like a stunt diver. Pretty soon it shot upward trailing white smoke. Quickly it formed a giant A in the sky. Next an M. Nothing for a few moments. There was a tentative cheer from the audience. Then it dove down making an 'I' spelling A-M-I. It started up to try to make a big E to finish the spelling in French of the word "friend." By now the crowd good-naturedly booed. The small plane waggled its wings and erased the letter I and the disfigured letter E. Immediately it sent out white smoke to make a small V with a tail. Finally A-M-Y. The crowd went wild.

****

When he got back to his hotel room, Norman needed to distract himself from their teary scene at the airport when Ricky left to go back to Richmond. He had walked her all the way to her gate and he wasn't sure which of them was more morose. Deep hugs and kisses to the point where the gate agent finally had to tap Norman on the shoulder and say, "She'd better go on board, because they're closing the door of the airplane right now."

He hung around until the Delta plane was headed for the runway.

In his room he got out his sketchbook. There were endless images that came to mind that he could draw – the front of the Richelieu's mansion, the little ferry that crossed the Mississippi to Algiers, the Richelieu's river boat, the balloon float, The Moors plantation house. Well into the evening he made six drawings. In some cases he added lots of detail and others were rough sketches. But he wasn't satisfied. Then he drew the parts of the Secret Garden, like the bougainvillea arbor and the gazebo. Finally it hit him. Norman took great care in drawing a beautiful magnolia blossom. It filled the page and was so realistic he smiled to think he could catch a faint aroma of that treasured flower – even though it was only paper. He propped the drawing up on the bed and then the desk. He was very pleased with himself.

Then another idea hit him. He opened the desk drawer in his room and got out a hotel envelope and writing paper. "Dearest, dearest Ricky, when I got back from the airport, I felt so lonely. Food didn't seem interesting at all. I tried but couldn't sleep. So I got to work on some sketches. You know me. I did quite a few. I want to show them to you when we are together again. They helped me remember what a fabulous time we had together. I spent a lot of time on the sketches of the Secret Garden. But the one I like the best is enclosed. I don't know about you, but I will never be able to look at a magnolia blossom again and not think of our time in the Secret Garden. Do magnolia trees grow in Richmond? Because if they do, I want to plant one when I get back. I can't wait to see you and hold you again. I love you, Norman."3

Boulder 1975

So this is what happened

One blustery day in September there was a note in Matt's hospital mailbox asking him to report to the General in charge of the Lackland Army Hospital the next Thursday at two in the afternoon.

They had checked his schedule and knew he was off on Thursday afternoons. He felt a slight rush of anxiety since when he asked around nobody at the hospital had been called before the General that they knew of. He told Janell that evening and she was puzzled as well. "Heck. No need to worry until we know what it's about," was her response. She was right, but nevertheless for several days Matt mulled over in his mind possible topics the General might want to speak with him about. He knew his work at the hospital was earning the highest possible evaluations. But there was the Boulder incident and that gnawed at him.

At the appointed time, Matt sat in the General's outer office. Flags and battle banners hung everywhere. He admired the deep wood paneling, the handsome furniture, and the efficient receptionist. However, these distractions did little to help with his anxiety. Finally the receptionist called him to follow her into the General's office.

It was furnished much the same way as the outer office – lots of wood paneling, flags all over the office – except there was a huge desk with just a few sheets of paper visible. Adjacent to it was what seemed like a massive bookcase indicating, perhaps, that the General was well read. When Matt glanced quickly he noted Winston Churchill was well represented along with a string of books about American presidents – Nixon, Kennedy, Theodore Roosevelt.

General Chester Burns came around the desk and greeted Matt without any warmth. As Matt expected, there was a large array of medals and ribbons on the General's left breast and he seemed quite tall – towering as a matter of fact – also as expected. He signaled Matt to join him at a casual seating area to the left of his desk with four chairs and a coffee table between them.

He held a thick manila envelope. "This is a serious matter. As with most of our interns, we are very interested in their backgrounds." Here Matt took in a deep breath as he imagined what was coming next. "I see you were an excellent student at Tufts, graduating with honors. But we also see that several years ago you were arrested and tried for a criminal charge."

Matt took a very deep breath. So that was it. He tried to smile, which was impossible. The General's question wasn't expected. He didn't respond for several minutes while trying to figure out the best way to tackle this very touchy subject. The pain he thought he had buried flashed back in his gut.

He thought for a bit more before he carefully responded, "You know I was found innocent at trial if you're referring to the Boulder incident?"

"Yes. I see that by the record, but we in medicine at Lackland want to hear it all from your perspective. It is about trust. Great medicine requires great trust. And I want to make sure we can have that trust by hearing it all from you."

Matt shrugged and hesitatingly said, "This is still very painful for me. And for it to make sense to you, I will need to give you quite a bit of background. It goes back to when I was an undergraduate in the 1970s. It's complicated and can be confusing at times. I need to emphasize that the whole incident revolved around a psychopath who targeted me, which makes it more difficult to sort out. And I will have to get you a recording made by this – what could I call him but a nutcase – that was discovered during the trial and was the basis of finding me innocent. Are you sure you want all the details?"

General Burns nodded.

Matt began. If General Burns wanted it all, he would spell it all out.

"In my sophomore year in Boulder in 1975, on my way out the door of my dorm room one day, I noticed a hunk of crumpled paper pushed up against the bookcase. I'm usually pretty neat so that was unusual, but I was in a hurry so I snatched it up and decided to see what it was when I returned. On my way to class, though, the crumpled paper somehow stuck with me and I assumed whatever it was, it probably got pushed over to the bookcase as I opened my door last evening."

Matt explained that he was headed on his bike for the east campus of the University of Colorado, which was about two miles from the central Boulder campus. His destination was a sizable, but secretive building. Even its name – the New Center for Science Innovation – wasn't evident anywhere. Many assumed it was funded by the federal government because of the hush-hush nature of its work. He was reminded in several emails about how very prestigious it is to be chosen for NCSI. Here high achieving students in engineering, math, chemistry, biology, physics and numerous other fields, along with comparable faculty, were brought together to try to figure out some of the toughest challenges the Center had been given by the federal government.

Matt pointed out to General Burns that, as he was aware, clearance by the FBI – just to be considered for NCSI – was intense and Matt was surprised at how deeply his background was checked. His father called one day to ask why some of his childhood neighbors were contacted to speak to the FBI about his character; to report that the now elderly Mr. Gruber, his high school English teacher, had been terribly frightened when the FBI called on him for a reference for Matt; why some of his coaches and dozens of others had been contacted by the FBI. Matt explained it was all part of his hope to work for a secret think tank on campus. "Dad, you always said, 'go for the best,' and this program is by far and away the best use of my brains I could ever ask for."

"My trek out to NCSI was stopped, however, when I got to the bike rack outside my dorm and was surprised to see my bike tires slashed. I looked up and down the row of about 40 other bikes and only mine were ruined. I was running a bit late and the unreliable campus shuttle wasn't a solution because it could make me really late. I had to get to NCSI on time. What a quandary. Take a taxi? Rent a car? Just then my friend from next door in my dorm came out the front door and I rushed to see if I could borrow his bike to make a mad dash for NCSI."

"Yeah, sure. I just need it back by seven tonight."

"I was out of breath and a bit sweaty and just made it through three security barriers around the NCSI building to join the ten other students who were at NCSI to take the last of four grinding exams. The results would admit only about six of the ten of us to the program. To say it was competitive would be underplaying the heavy stress we were under. It was the prestige (four Genius Awards with a $500,000 stipend for any kind of research in only six years of NCSI's existence) and financial benefits (pay of $20,000 annually for each of the chosen students) that drove us.

"Once I got there this man said, 'Welcome again to NCSI. My name is Evan. Before we get to the exam room, I have been asked to give you a tour of three of the projects assigned to NCSI and so here are the same Top Secret badges you were assigned last time. Please sign the non-disclosure statements on this clipboard, and remember, any mention to anyone of anything of what you see today will mean your immediate dismissal entirely from this university – not just this program, but from the university. No appeal. No second chance. NCSI is very serious about this.'

Evan told us that while the number of faculty, staff and students cleared to work inside the building was quite small – probably no more than 45 – for about two months there had been leaks about some of the work taking place at NCSI. He went on to say, "Specifically, on our visit today we'll visit three NCSI projects. First we'll go to a lab where a team is working on procedures for handling a worldwide pandemic of bird flu and/or swine flu. This project has many elements – from medical, to engineering, logistics and even communications. Second, we'll inspect some very sophisticated work being done on fingerprints. In the world of terrorism, fingerprinting has become a very big problem with the ability of some groups to actually transfer prints – using the newest digital means – of innocent people. We will also look at some of the special fire and force protection suits being designed to protect state department officials at overseas embassies when a riot or building invasion breaks out suddenly. After that we'll go to the exam room you're familiar with by now for the final test for admittance."

****

Matt explained he was exhausted when he returned to his dorm room after the exam. He thought about the crumpled paper, but in his tiredness, he slumped onto his bed with the envelope unread in his hand.

Over his morning coffee, he carefully unfolded the paper and inside read, "You sat next to me at the NCSI exam. I saw you glance at my paper on at least half a dozen times. That's cheating. I am sure something dangerous is going on at NCSI – something I don't trust. When I tried to ask what goes on out there, they went blank and that makes me furious as it is. If I don't make it into the program, I'm going after you because you are a cheater. The least I will do is have my lawyer file a complaint with the Chancellor and the police accusing you of cheating. If that doesn't work, I may go far beyond that. There are lots of things I am willing to do to get what I want. Revenge is my motive." It was signed NB.

"That seemed so bizarre to me. Was this some kind of crazy person writing a note like this?

"I was stunned. I had never, ever cheated my whole time in school much less been accused of cheating. For the life of me, I couldn't even remember who sat next to me for the NCSI exam, much less someone with the initials NB. No face came to mind. Not a thing. I sat for a long time deciding what to do. I started a letter to the Chancellor's office thinking I could make a pre-emptive move and go to the Chancellor with NB's note and defend myself; somehow try to find NB and confront him about his false accusation, or I could do nothing. Most drastic of all – I could drop out of the competition for a NCSI spot. The last option, however, was not even remotely possible. I did not give up, especially for something as specious as a false accusation of cheating from someone I did not know."

He told the General the situation got more worrisome

after the list of successful NCSI candidates was posted and emailed the following day and there was Matt at number three. There was no one with the initials NB.

"When I opened my dorm room door late that day, there was another white envelope. I saw it as soon as I opened my door and without hesitating opened it. 'Nice going. You are in and I am out. Watch for my next move, cheater. I will do about anything to seek justice somehow. It may mean bringing down the whole NCSI thing. Believe me, I have the means to get what I want. You will be toast. NB'"

After reading the note he said he felt his underarms grow damp, something that seldom happened except when he was under heavy duress. He wasn't sure if it was the heat or the note or both, but it made him very uncomfortable. Instead of being elated at his NCSI acceptance, he was depressed by it. How could he be excited by the challenges ahead with this hanging over him? Was this guy serious? The second note made him seem more like a lunatic than the first one. He sat for a long time just staring at the opposite wall.

"I knew I should do something about this note – just because it was such a threat to me and the NCSI program, but I kind of shoved it out of my mind and in the weeks that followed I put my head down anyway and relished the work at NCSI. Now I know I shouldn't have, but I forgot about NB and became immersed in the work I was assigned. My unit leader explained the very challenging work we would tackle for the State Department in protecting its people against all dangers. And there were plenty of dangers. Our specific unit was charged with developing a fire and force resistant suit with corresponding shoes, gloves and headgear. It sounded relatively simple, but proved very difficult given the pages of government requirements for lightness, flexibility, weight and speed. Probably the most difficult part of the whole exercise was to design the pieces so the potential wearer could be in all the protective gear in less than a minute.

"In a high-walled, non-secure but cavernous outside storage area of the NCSI building, carpenters built a fake concrete wall patterned after the actual windows and doors in the Karachi embassy in Pakistan. An outside crew was recruited to storm the fake walls and start an instantaneous fire. With the help of the Boulder Fire Department, we tested and re-tested about a dozen suits made of various materials. One time I suited up and walked unharmed through a wall of flames while my unit mates checked gauges and dials to measure every possible move. I was unharmed, but this suit was considered a failure because the heat transferred into the suit was stifling. My colleagues and I spent the next two months working with fabric designers to attempt to bring down the heat factor. The chest protector proved a big hurdle to cooling down the suit. And our progress was very slow because of the secrecy of the project. Periodically a handful of students and faculty working at NCSI gathered in the auditorium where one or two of the teams were assigned to make presentations of their work. For some reason I was chosen to demonstrate on a Wednesday afternoon the speed at which I could get into all the fire and force retardant trappings. There was a huge wall clock with seconds clicking off as I grabbed the suit and I began the process of covering myself. I could see the clock but not hear any conversation, which was stifled by my thick headgear." Matt paused and then continued.

"In mid-presentation what I did hear – with absolute, frightening clarity – was a huge blast. Suddenly parts of the room flew everywhere. Chairs and other furniture were being thrown against walls. Pipes had ruptured and water was fountaining through the air. The wall clock came whirling at me like a big disc. Searching my mind for what was going on, my first thought was that this might be our supervisors' way of springing a real live demo without telling us, but then I caught a glance of one of my team mates lying at my feet with blood flowing from a head gash and a large hole in his chest. I looked around for someone to help but it was impossible to see exactly what was going on in the confusion. What really shook me was when I looked up toward the seating area where my colleagues and teachers were seated and they all were motionless, like a row of mummies covered in thick dust. I could not tell if they might even have perished. There was another explosion that blew out what looked like a huge opening in the windowless wall of the auditorium. Then a wall of fire engulfed the whole room, and I have enough experience in science to know it might cause another immediate explosion encouraged by the new source of oxygen flowing in through the hole."

Matt shuddered at the thought of this memory.

"I looked out the gap, and saw, incongruously, a tranquil scene of grass and hedges and flower beds outside, and then I felt a strange, painful warming in my right leg and my neck. Then the pain in both areas became more intense and as I glanced down I saw a hole had been ripped in the leg of my hazmat coveralls. It was very apparent that my suit protective had failed at this point and hesitatingly, I felt down and touched a blistering burn where my skin had been torched. I took a step and almost fell into a tangle of bent furniture. When I tried to turn my head to take in the scene away from the wall to calculate whether I could help any of my colleagues, I couldn't as pain shot through my whole head and neck. For some reason I dared not touch my neck injury. Instinctively I took a step toward the open wall, stumbled forward and fell. Now the wound on my right leg was so painful, I felt I might not be able to get up. But I did, sensing I had no alternative but to somehow make it to the outside world."

****

"The front page picture in the Boulder paper the next morning had an eight column color photo that showed me pitching through what they said was a car-sized hole with a ring of fire surrounding me. As it happened, I managed to get a few feet from the building and fell onto the grass in my full regalia. The worst part was the paper also reported that three of my NCSI colleagues had perished in the explosions and fires. What that photo couldn't show was the expression of deep pain on my face. It was for both what I thought were my lost colleagues and for the serious burns and pain in my leg and neck.

****

"To say I was devastated isn't close to what I was feeling. I felt hollow. Except for the terrible pain in my right leg, there was a numb feeling in the rest of me. At the hospital they were great. The doctor treating the burns on my leg and neck was my hero. He said there was a big problem because, besides the leg burn, I had somehow broken my leg at the same time. He was hopeful, but at the same time I had to accept the fact I might have a permanent limp. He was adamant, however, that with good physical therapy the limp might go away. My neck wound would leave a noticeable scar even with several skin grafts, according to my doctor. I guessed I could live with those, but my mental state had gone downhill. There seemed to be a lot of people who wanted to see me. I kept thinking it was more out of curiosity than anything else. Janell, a girl from Boston I had dated for several months, called and left repeated offers to come and talk. I never returned her calls. I just couldn't. A grief counselor came to my hospital room one afternoon, knocked very softly and spoke in a soothing voice, but I sent her away. It got worse when among the string of people at my door were two FBI agents who appeared after three days and asked me to come down to police to headquarters – when I was able – for questioning. It would be friendly they said, but my nerves were in such a condition I wasn't sure how I could make it downtown, much less face a bunch of inquisitors.

"When I got out of the hospital, probably the most difficult part of the horrible NCSI incident was the memorial service on the main university campus. The several acres of green lawn that stretched from the library at one end of the quadrangle to the biology building at the other end were jammed with somber people. I had been asked to sit in the front row in case I wanted to say something, but I knew that would never happen. As I started to sit I saw the parents – a few rows back – of one of my friends who had died. And over on the edge of the seats was the sister of another colleague who died in the explosion. She was convulsed in tears. After that I couldn't even look up, but stared at the grass around my feet. I did take notice that just before the program got underway a body slid into an empty chair next to me. I glanced sideways. It was Janell. Somehow that made me feel a bit better.

"After the lengthy service was over, she asked if I wanted company and just then I really did. Where could we go? Could I hobble on my crutches over to Owens Coffee Shop? The Hilltopper Restaurant? If I wanted to avoid people, she suggested a room where they could have privacy in the Alpha Phi sorority house, just across the street. This woman was so great as she listened to my woes. I told her I hadn't been to class in several weeks, so I guessed – even though I haven't formally withdrawn – that I was no longer a student at the University of Colorado. And NCSI is finished. They sent me a letter telling me it would be better if I stayed away – for a while at least. They would let me know if and when to return. The investigation into what happened was dragging on. What to do next? I kept asking myself 'what's next?' And frankly I had no idea. Maybe the Army – if my injury doesn't keep me out – if they'll have me.

"Janell told me something like, 'That's nonsense. You didn't do anything wrong. Why not speak with someone at the university and see if your class schedule can be put back together so you can continue – if that's what you want.'

"So I told her that I wasn't sure what I wanted to do. I knew I didn't do anything wrong, but the day before I sat down with Janell, the Boulder Police came to my dorm room and said they had new evidence and could I come to the station tomorrow for more questioning. That was a little scary. I had no idea what was going on with the investigation but I figured I would find out at the police station.

****

"Instead of being accommodated and led into the Chief's office like I was the first time, I was invited to come down to police headquarters. This time I was shown into an interrogation room like the ones you see in TV crime shows. Gray walls. Just two chairs, one on each side of a gray table. It seemed better lit than those in the TV cop shows. I did notice two tall cans in the middle of the table. Without touching them, I looked at one of the canisters that appeared to have been severely scorched in a fire. I noticed most of the labeling was destroyed as I looked very closely to see if I could decipher the chemical contents. In my careful examination of the canister, I noted what I thought were two labels – one for ant poison covering another for fire booster. That seemed very strange to me.

"Soon a plain clothes man came into the room and introduced himself as Detective Jameson, who said he was the lead detective on the NCSI case and would be questioning me this afternoon. His first gesture was to shove one of the canisters toward me."

"Ever seen this before?"

"I stared and said nothing. I was surprised at the question and with the tension now rising in the room, I could feel dampness beginning under my arms. I don't even drink canned soda, so no, this type of can was unfamiliar to me. I told the detective 'It looks like it's been in a fire though.'

"He told me, 'In combing through the wreckage of the NCSI auditorium digging for clues, the expert fire detectives from Denver and the FBI came across this canister which was found right next to a 500 gallon oxygen tank that exploded. This is a high-powered fire enhancer that apparently was placed around the tank and the investigation noted this product caused the huge explosion that killed your colleagues and destroyed a portion of NCSI. The National Park Service usually uses this product when they start controlled fires in various parks and forests around the country. To start a fire, the rangers don't just strike a match to get it started. It's my understanding they use something like this to create an explosive fire.'

"I told him, 'Okay, I see the fire booster part of the damaged label, but another portion says it is for ant poison. What is that about? And what does that have to do with me?'

"A lot."

"At this point in my up and down emotional state, I started to get mad. Then I quickly calmed down and said, 'Okay, why does it have anything to do with me when I've never seen such a product – ever? And what's with the two labels? That makes it very confusing.'"

"His answer was, 'Your fingerprints were found on the canister. They were very clear.'"

"I didn't need this new jolt after what I'd been through the past few weeks. I asked, 'Can you say that again? I am stunned because I have never, ever seen such a can before, much less used anything like that stuff. Sure, I've used fire starter on a barbecue, but never anything like this.'"

"In his best cop way, he told me this discovery has changed the whole investigation." He said, "The change is that at this point you are the prime suspect. You can remain silent, but you better get a lawyer. And we suggest you take a lie-detector test."

"That was unexpected. One of my closest friends had to take one a few months ago and he told me to be careful because some testers can be trusted better than others. I recall he told me to stay away from a certain company – I think it's called 'Mountain West Testing Service' – because he learned they can be swayed – and as it turned out in his case that's exactly what happened.

"I felt I could ask the detective who would be conducting the lie detector test and he said 'Mountain West Testing.' So my response was, 'No.'"

"The detective stared at me with the fiercest look I imagined he could come up with. 'Did you just refuse?' he asked. My response was "I did. I want some other company."

"I just made it back to my dorm after the police meeting. As soon as I got close to the front door another shocker greeted me as I had to hobble through a gauntlet of news people asking questions and shoving microphones in my face. 'Prime witness…Fingerprints on a can of fire…Get a lawyer.' All were very frightening thoughts. Janell called and left several messages. I heeded not one of them.

"After two days of people at my door knocking loudly

and beseeching me to come out and speak with them, the situation calmed down and after a while there was a gentle knock and the voice said, 'Matt. It's Janell. We need to talk.'

"I didn't move at first. The knock came again, gently, and I got up on shaky legs and went to the door. I covered my unshaven face as she came in carrying a package. I was in shambles. Janell didn't say a word at first. I sat in the chair at my desk and she on my bed. Not a word for a long time. And then she got up and came over and started to massage my shoulders. I remember I gave a slight twist away at first, but then I started to relax. She was the first to speak as she continued massaging. 'I'm not going to be nice. You need to get yourself out of this slump, this poor me thing, Matt, because you've got bigger challenges ahead. At this point you're caving in and that won't work. Believe me.'

"She told me, 'You probably haven't read a newspaper or seen TV or turned on the radio. Have you? So I'm sure you don't know what the Boulder District Attorney has planned.' I shook my head. She told me to prepare myself because it was announced that day that the DA was setting up a Grand Jury. She told me I would have to appear before the Grand Jury as a witness without an attorney.

"The Grand Jury may take weeks questioning many witnesses, but if at the end of their term they return an indictment, that means you will be formally charged and your case will go to trial," Janell continued. "You will need an attorney regardless. Hope you don't mind but I have spoken with someone I know at the law school – she's a part time instructor with a thriving practice downtown – about whether she would take on your case pro bono. I don't have an answer yet, but she seemed positive. Said she would get back to me tomorrow which is good because you need counsel right away."

"It was a lot to digest," Matt said. "And that reality – the thought of going before a Grand Jury – hit me and so I stood up, bit into the apple on my desk and went to my bathroom for a much-needed shower."

****

"If you've ever been in the Grand Jury room, it's quite an experience. Especially in Boulder where you have a bunch of pretty capable people such as university professors, writers, healthcare professionals and the like. Back and forth with the DA trying his best to rattle me. One of his questions was, 'You told the Boulder Police that no, you would not take a lie detector test. Is that correct?' My response was 'No. That is not correct. I said I would not take the test from a company I understand can be swayed. I would take a test from another company. I did not say I wouldn't take a lie detector test."

****

"After the Grand Jury returned an indictment against me, the Boulder County DA took the case himself. He bore down on me unmercifully."

Q. "We went back in your record and found that when you were 12 years old, you and a friend started a fire near your home in Brookline, Massachusetts that burned about half an acre of woods. Is that true?"

A. "It is true"

Q. "Was your motivation for the NCSI fire to settle a dispute with another student?"

A. "That is just not true. I had absolutely no reason to start a fire of any kind."

Q. "Why were you the only one wearing the protective hazmat suit?"

A. "It was an assigned demonstration. The choice for someone to demonstrate the suit wasn't mine to make."

Q. "Did you cheat on any of the NCSI tests?"

A. "Absolutely not."

Q. "One other thing we found in your record had to do with the university's gigantic Flaming C bonfire before the annual homecoming game. In your freshman year the fire got out of control and the campus police accused you and some of your roommates of throwing fire accelerant into the bonfire. That's when the fire jumped to a temporary fence and nearly burned down the Hagardy Alumni Center. Did you have anything to do that?"

A. "Sir. If you had read the follow-up investigative report, you would have noted that I was completely cleared of any involvement with that fire."

****

"And so it went. My attorney Caroline Peacock and I huddled each day after court to plan strategy and anticipate what might come next. One night on a whim I rummaged through a drawer where I keep miscellaneous papers I don't know what to do with. Amazingly, in all the junk, I turned up the second threatening note from NB and the next day excitedly brought it to show Caroline. We talked about this note from NB and about the first one I could not find, but Caroline didn't think they would prove much. She said NB sounded slightly deranged, but how would they ever find such a person with the initials NB? NCSI had proved to be totally unhelpful in the few inquiries she had made there. They emphatically said they would not cooperate. And the FBI followed that up with a letter to Caroline saying the same thing because of the secrecy of the entire operation.

"But somehow the note bothered Caroline. It seemed

slightly off-kilter and clearly threatening. Her husband was a dean at the university and so she asked if he had any ideas on how she might track down such a person in a university of 30,000 students. He gave her an idea, albeit a chancy one. He told her, 'You know the head of the Student Counseling Service on campus. This unknown person certainly sounds like he needs lots of counseling, so why not try to track this person down that way? Who knows? He might have shown up there. But there may be a client-privacy issue. But I would pursue it. Frankly we want to find out too since the university could be involved as it was a year ago when that other crazy student shot up the theater in Broomfield.'

"Before court Caroline made a call to her friend Maddy. As she was pretty sure, her SCS contact declined to provide any information to Caroline citing client privilege. So Caroline tried a different tack. 'Let me ask this. What if there was a report in your files of a psychotic student who made any kind of threat with the initials NB? Let's say you never counseled this person, but just had a report. Would that be privileged?'

"Let me think about that and I'll get back to you. But here's a suggestion. Check with the Boulder Police too, because they may have something on this character."

****

Matt was exhausted at this point and turned to the General and said, "This is long. Do you want to hear more?'" And in his most military-speak voice he said, "I want it all."

Matt dove back into his account of his trying experience at Boulder.

"Okay. At mid-morning in court the next day, Caroline's assistant Joni approached the defense attorney table and handed her boss a note that indicated that she had some blockbuster information from the Boulder Police. Because Joni had worked for her for so long and she had such credibility, Caroline decided to take a definite risk and so she stood and said to the judge, 'Your Honor, I hate to break into the proceedings, but I have just learned of some new evidence that might possibly change the course of this trial, so can we take a ten minute break while my assistant and I confer with you?'"

Matt stopped for a moment to remember what happened next.

"Apparently in chambers Joni reported that the police department called their law office that morning. She took the call and they told her something startling. Apparently the police dispatcher got a call at 8:40 a.m. from a caller who would only identify himself as NB. He wouldn't give his full name. That was how he identified himself. It was a long rambling call. Her notes summarizing what he said were, 'I got my revenge. I brought down NCSI and that kid Matt. They all deserved it. If you want to know all about how I did it, there is a tape in my warehouse at 9413 Superior Street. Tells it all. Come and get it.' Joni went on to report that after that phone call, the Boulder police had to break down the door at the warehouse address the caller gave on Superior Street. Once inside they could smell something strange. Also, there was a low rumble like one of the cars inside had been left running. In searching around for the identity of the person who made the call, one of the officers noticed a black hose running from the exhaust pipe of a shiny green Jaguar. They followed it and there in the driver's seat of the same car was a man with his head to one side and his tongue out. When the police forced open the car door and pulled the driver onto the floor, there was no pulse. Beside him on the seat was this tape. She said, 'I've only listened to a couple of minutes of it, but it's pretty weird.' In searching the Superior Street office, they discovered that NB were the initials of a man named Nicolas Bartlett.

"Furthermore, when the police ran that name through their system, it did turn up a report about a Nicolas Bartlett who made several threats about bombing people he felt did him wrong. The police apparently did nothing because they were only threats and never resulted in any harm. She put the report and the tape on the judge's desk for him to examine. Caroline told the judge they would need time to review this new material and if it could be verified, bring it to the court. After this short conference the judge recessed court to allow Caroline to review all the material and find any possible witnesses based on the report of Nicolas Bartlett."

****

"I was told that that evening that Caroline and Joni pored over the dense files and listened to a portion of the tape found by the police. They both had a distinct recognition – as they read and made notes – that this information would turn my case totally around. They discussed some of the highlights from the report in the police files: Nicolas Bartlett was the eldest son of Horace Bartlett, deceased billionaire owner of Bartlett Oil and Gas in Colorado Springs. Nicolas was brilliant with Phi Beta Kappa undergraduate and master's degrees in chemistry from Yale. For the past two years he had been enrolled off and on in a PhD program at the university in Boulder, attractive because of the Nobel Prize winning faculty members in the chemistry department.

"They said his enrollment was a mess because he could be unruly in class, seldom went to lab or turned in papers on time and used his considerable brainpower to brush off any assignment he didn't like. Because of this range of odd behaviors, the university suspended Nicolas from time to time and then took him back since his trust fund held a third of his father's billions. He had a troubled youth with a litany of minor skirmishes with the law. None had resulted in any serious action because his father always had a flight of attorneys quash any problems Nicolas had had over the years. But in the recent past, there had been a couple of troubling threats. One such threat was to blow up the football coach's office if he didn't get the season tickets he wanted. Nothing came of that. At another time, he had threatened a student for what Nicolas considered cheating. Apparently he had not followed through on that threat either. Because of those incidents, he was referred for help at the Student Counseling Service at the University of Colorado a number of times. They said he repeatedly would make an appointment and then not show up.

"Joni also came across three letters from Nicolas' mother tucked way back in the file that she sent to the Student Counseling Service after they asked for any information she had about her son. Each one seemed more desperate. In the first one she wrote that Nicolas had become obsessed with a fellow student in middle school after he felt that student had copied from Nicolas. 'He hounded this boy Charlie so much the parents got a restraining order. It was dreadful. And Charlie hadn't done anything. It was just more of Nicolas' hateful behavior.' In the final note she said she didn't want to admit that over the years her husband had beaten Nicolas repeatedly for not being manly enough. And he faced the same taunt in school too. She said she believed this caused him to feel people were out to get him. Joni discovered all of this information had been assembled into a report and provided to the Boulder Police Department primarily because of the threats. The tape was another story altogether. General. Shall I summarize because you can listen when you play the tape after I deliver it to you?"

"Okay. You can summarize, but I will still listen to every word once I have the tape."

"I'm not sure I can remember word-for-word what he said but here goes. 'This is a tape I want the world to know about because I got what I wanted out of it. The first thing I did was wait in the NCSI the parking lot until I saw a short man in coveralls head for a decrepit looking truck. Just before he started to open the door I approached and said, 'Hello. I'm NB. Are you a janitor here at NCSI? I ask because I'm looking for a part-time janitor for my warehouse. Tell me your name.' Caroline and Joni were astonished at the detail Nicolas recorded. They both couldn't decide whether he was egotistical or delusional, but they agreed that he seemed suicidal. Joni then asked, 'Even though the tape isn't finished do you think we have enough information to go back to the judge for a dismissal?'

****

"Well into the night, Caroline and Joni found new information and discussed their new strategy based on these files and the tape, and they began to feel sure it would prove I was not guilty, if Caroline handled it right.

"According to what was found toward midnight Joni said, 'It's bothered me for some time that Nicolas would take such draconian action against Matt and NCSI just for supposed cheating on an exam. It's unbalanced, but that's him. But I think I came across the answer in one of his mother's letters to the Student Counseling Service.'

"She was referring to the note Nicolas' mother wrote about when her son became obsessed with Charlie, a student in middle school, supposedly over some plagiarism. He harassed and bullied Charlie to the point where the parents got a TRO."

****

Matt told the General that in the courtroom a day later, Caroline asked to approach the bench since she had a new witness that could potentially change the whole direction of the trial. She held up a tape recording.

"Mr. Chavez, please state your name and then please you tell this courtroom how you became involved with the terrible explosion at NCSI?

"Manuel wept as he related his relationship with Mr. Bartlett. 'My name is Manuel Chavez. One day after work this man approached me in the parking lot where I work at NCSI. He said he needed a part-time janitor at his business downtown. We talked. Then he mentioned he would pay me $25 an hour for 10 hours a week, working to clean his old cars in his warehouse near downtown. I couldn't believe it because that was more than double what I was making at NCSI. I told him 'That's good. Real good 'cause I got seven kids. And one is going to school at the university. No money.'

"Caroline said, 'Please continue.'

"This man invited me to his warehouse after dinner that day and said we could talk more about his projects – where I might help him. He said the address was 9413 Superior Street. I'll never forget him saying, 'And by the way, if we do work together, there may be enough money for you to buy a new van, so you can get rid of your old truck and take all your family to picnics, the movies, wherever.' I was so happy."

"Then what happened?" Caroline asked.

"I went to his warehouse at 7:30 that night. When I got inside all I could say was, 'Wow. I never knew this was here.' He invited me to follow him over to his desk. He said, 'I try not to show off when it comes to advertising on this building. No signs outside because I don't want anybody bothering me. But as you can see from the inside sign above my desk, we're serious about our pest control business. We have several contracts with big companies in town and the university – to help them get rid of bad bugs.'

"I told him, 'I know about that. My boss is always complaining about our bug problem where I work at NCSI.'"

Matt remembered, "At this point Manuel started to cry again."

"I took in cans that said ant poison. I never knew that hidden inside the cans was such a terrible thing that would kill people. I wouldn't have done anything like that – on my own. Mr. Bartlett was so nice to me and helped me support my family. He gave me a job. He paid me enough money so that I could get rid of my junker truck and buy my family a van. He gave me lots of money. But now I know he was a very bad man."

"And so it went. Caroline moved for dismissal of the charges against me and I was declared innocent by the judge. I was free. God, I was happy."

****

In the General's office, it was well into the evening when Matt finished talking. "And that, General Burns, is perhaps more information than you wanted to know about the Boulder incident. I can't emphasize enough that I was found innocent of all charges. It would have been nice if everything had gone back to normal after that. But, honestly, it took me months to shake off the emotional roller coaster I had been on. That's when I decided not to go back to school right away and instead joined the Army. I believe I have to say my maturity took a huge leap when I went from being a college student one day to being an indicted criminal in a very short period of time. And to go through all of that knowing I was innocent..."

To end the conversation the general said, "Dr. Hudson. I have heard your part of the story. I will listen to the tape when I get it. Whatever my advisory group and I decide will be final. Please understand there is no appeal. Good night to you." The general's receptionist had gone home by then, so Matt had to find his own way out.

****

Matt made sure the next day to deliver to General Burns the tape Nicolas made of his dreadful actions. That evening the general sat in his study at home and went through the tape. It was scratchy at times, but compelling.

When the General was about halfway through the recording, the housekeeper tapped gingerly on his study door and said his wife was in the dining room and she asked if he wanted to take a break for some dinner? His response was, "I thought I told you never to interrupt me when I'm in here. Tell my wife I'll be there when I'm ready."

At dinner his wife said she heard voices from the study. "What is that all about? Did you have some people in there?"

"Of course not. Nobody goes in my study except me. You know that. I was listening to a tape recording." Then he was silent as he ate his dinner of pork chops and au gratin potatoes. He didn't say another word during dinner and went back to his study to listen to the rest of the tape.

Back in his study after dinner, when he switched on the machine again, this is what the rest of the recorded message said...

"Manuel nodded knowingly, 'I know about that. My boss

is always complaining about our bug problem where I work at NCSI.' "

"Oh really, I responded. Maybe Superior can help. But more about that later. Let's go over to the cars."

"I let Manuel wander among the Jaguars in my warehouse. He had never seen anything like this display before. He admired the chrome, the paint, the leather seats, the convertible tops. 'Can I touch?' And I let him admire 10 of my cars.

"I told him that they required a lot of cleaning and a thorough cleaning every spring. I knew he was all for it so I sealed the deal by offering him $25 an hour in cash, which would equate to about $1,000 a month. I offered him bonuses. I told him he could start that week. I gave him a wad of cash upfront, too. After he left, I couldn't believe my genius. Now I could put a check mark against the last part of my scheme. Well, not quite yet, but soon. Then I sat at his computer and got creative. At the top of the page I wrote, 'Contract, between National Center for Science Innovation and Superior Pest Control. For Pest Control.'

"The transfer onto the labels was taken care of by NCSI student Blair Nottage, the ultimate fingerprint expert. He had proved easier to handle than I thought. As I knew, money was the answer. I showered lots of cash on Blair.

"Eventually I advanced my plan with Manual, without his knowledge. I brought out the contract and told him my company was hired by NCSI to help eradicate their bug problem. I told him my experience with him had been very good. I explained that the eradication program is clear-cut: take in the canisters over a period of time; place them exactly where I require; let them do their job. I don't even need to be there. You might check on them now and then – and that's it. Oh, and as my partner you will earn half the $50,000 fee.

"Manual couldn't believe it. He said something like, 'Do you really mean I could earn $25,000?' I sold him on it by

telling him he could now buy a house, send his other kids to college, he ate it all up. He said, 'Oh Mr. Nicolas. I've never thought about that much money. I don't think I can accept it. It's too much.' But he accepted anyway. So I instructed him to pick up six selected Superior Pest Control cans to be placed exactly as I dictated. Security should not be a problem because Manuel had all the necessary clearances. And if there was a question, he could just show the guards the Superior contract. What Manuel didn't know was each of the cans had a thin wire attached that could be accessed on a frequency available only to me. When Manuel left, I couldn't help pumping my arms in the air..."

After listening to it all the way through, the General thought the tape long, but noted it was authenticated by the Boulder Police Department.

****

Matt and Janell put Matt's visit with the General out of their minds. But two weeks after that session a letter arrived addressed to Matt. He read it quickly, then aloud to Janell.

It was dated September 25, 1984 and said, "Dear Dr. Hudson: My Advisory Group and I have carefully reviewed the information you gave me including all the files and the tape. The conclusion we have come to is that trust is paramount in medicine and therefore we feel it would be better for you to transfer to another medical facility outside the military. This has nothing to do with your skills as a physician. If you want, I have arranged for you to continue your internship at a civilian hospital in Laredo, Texas. I have a friend there who will help settle you and your wife in Laredo. The Army will pay your tuition, fees and a salary, just as though you had stayed here at Lackland. In addition, you will be given an Honorable Discharge from the Army and will be able to draw a pension at the appropriate age. All of this is conditioned on your telling no one of this arrangement. If you are in agreement, please sign below and return the original of this letter to me."

Matt was disappointed, but he had been through a lot, so he wasn't shocked. Matt and Janell went out for dinner. Matt told Janell that he didn't feel as badly as he thought he should given the nonsense of the General's decision. "What do you think?"

Janell waited a bit to answer. "Heck, we've been through worse before. You've got a job. You can continue your internship. Honorable Discharge. Why not?"

He loved this woman intensely and told her. Then, "Actually I'm pretty happy. Now I won't have to deal with all that military nonsense anymore. I wonder what Laredo is like?"

Laredo September 1984

The bad people appear

In their tiny kitchen in Lackland base housing Janell was reading through some of the literature she had sent for about Laredo. For Matt's benefit she said, "You know, it doesn't look as bad as we thought – for Texas. Lots of events and festivals. Maybe those will be fun. This will probably interest you. They have a huge country music festival soon after we get there. On another note, I don't quite understand why they celebrate George Washington's birthday for the whole month of February. Seems incongruous, but I guess we'll find out. Other than that it looks like another dry, desert town in Texas. Fairly big though. The population is around 240,000 people. Oh, I am sure this will also interest you. Laredo is the only city in America that has been under seven different flags – France, Spain, Mexico, its own Republic, Texas, the Confederacy and finally the USA."

Matt was busy making his famous huevos rancheros in anticipation of their soon being very close to Mexico. "Thanks for all that. I've done some of my own research on Laredo. From what I've learned so far, it is the main crossing between Mexico and the U.S. – I read they have four international bridges that span the Rio Grande because there's a ton of cheap labor across the border from Laredo. I read Nuevo Laredo is Mexico's main manufacturing center and so there is a huge amount of goods crossing into the US over those bridges.

"I wonder about drugs crossing at that point too. Without knowing anything about the drug trade down there, it could be huge. I also read there have been gun fights right in Laredo over drugs – between the cartels – or something like that."

Janell got up and came over to Matt at the stove. She stood behind him and reached around his waist. "That doesn't sound good. Are you sure you – we – want to go down there?"

Without turning away from his cooking, Matt said, "The good news is the medical facilities are top-notch. I'm not sure why, but the hospital I will intern at – South Texas Medical Center – is a teaching hospital with over 300 beds. They also do a considerable amount of research, which means the hospital will have professionals and facilities not found in many other places. I still have to do more of my own research on the STMC, as they call it, but initially it looks pretty good. I've also learned their Trauma Center is very active – probably more active than other ERs in a city the size of Laredo – because it serves both sides of the border. I say with a certain amount of trepidation, let's hope that isn't due to drug dealers shooting themselves and others. But that's not mine to judge. In my profession we treat them all."

After breakfast Janell got out three pictures of the rental the realtor had sent her that they were moving to in Laredo. "Looks kind of cute. Small, but we don't need much space." She handed the photos to Matt who looked them over quickly. His mind was still on STMC.

****

Since their house was in South Laredo on a cul de sac, Matt and Janell soon got to know their neighbors. Buddy Romer and his wife Rachel came over to introduce themselves the second day after Matt and Janell had moved in. In typical Texas hospitality style, they brought a lot of food – a big casserole, home baked bread and a bunch of chocolate cupcakes. Interestingly, Buddy was a border patrolman and he filled them in – as much as he was allowed – on their questions about the drug trade.

They were on Matt and Janell's back patio drinking iced tea.

"I hate to say it but as an ER doc, you may very well be involved with some victims of drug gang violence that can spill over to this side of the border. Speaking for my department, we have added more people and have worked hard to be stricter with enforcement in the last few years, so I'm pleased to say we've seen a big drop in crime rates. But I am sure you know that the demand for drugs is so strong in America it's a constant battle. Maybe that's the wrong word, but you know what I mean. The creativity in smuggling drugs across is amazing. Just last month we broke up a drug ring that had organized the Rio Grande Miniature Sailing Club that had kids with toy boats holding races on the river. Nice, healthy activity for those kids – except the boats were laden with cocaine. Each boat – small as it was – could hold about $20,000 worth of coke. And let's not forget the four bridges we have in Laredo that go across the Rio Grande. They are a constant temptation for the bad guys," Buddy said.

The stories from Brad and Evelyn Whiting on the other side of their house were more upbeat since he was a broadcaster with the local NBC television station. The Whitings talked about the excellent education their kids were getting in the Laredo public schools – the high number of National Merit Scholars, for instance, that annually came out of such a small town. Comparatively, it was impressive that Laredo was third in the nation with its number of scholars on a per capita basis. But nonetheless, in some of their visits between the two houses, the drug trade came up now and then. Brad told them he reported recently on a woman who tried to cross the border after she had sewn crystal meth into her breast implants. "It was ugly. We couldn't use any visuals as you can imagine. It was a hard story. But one of many in Laredo."

One reason they chose the neighborhood where they settled was because it was only three miles from STMC. As was the case wherever he was, Matt was uncomfortable driving such a short distance and taking up parking at the medical center and so he began his pitch with Janell for a bicycle. He missed Traveler, but didn't say it to Janell because he knew she already knew. "You know they wouldn't allow me to have a bike at Lackland. But we're not there anymore. Not being able to have a bike may seem like a small matter, but it was part of a much bigger system – that whole military thing – that can be stifling. I need to stop right here and say how happy I am to be out from under all the military nonsense we saw at Lackland. I know I've ranted about this before, but in the short time I've been at STMC I'm convinced we deliver better medicine because we don't have that overlay of military hierarchy."

Janell was next. "I am amazed at that general at Lackland – what was his name, Chester Burns? – who sent you away over a horrendous incident in which you were found completely innocent. I initially was fine, even though it made no sense. It actually makes me a little angry, but I think we've come out of it for the better. As you say, you're out from under that 'military nonsense.' This house alone is a real treat compared with the sterile base housing we were in at Lackland. You're busy at the hospital, but I'm getting to know this town and I like it – except for the incredible heat – and, so far, the neighbors seem pretty nice. It all seems more relaxed."

"And need I remind us both," Matt said, "that we have all the benefits of the Army and none of the bad stuff. It was obvious Chester was covering his ass. Remember there were generals with more stars than his two above him and I believe he was afraid. In spite of his outward toughness, I think inside he was a chicken. Probably like a lot of his colleagues. Maybe we've got it wrong – we should celebrate General Chester Burns for doing what he did. Hooray!"

The conversation stopped for a few minutes. Matt began again, "Venting about the military distracted us from my bicycle talk. So on to more important things. My darling wife, are you okay with my getting another bicycle?" Matt waited. "I take your nod to mean 'go ahead.' I do wonder where Norman is with Traveler. I'd love to have it back. The last time I spoke with him he had a job in Richmond, Virginia and was using the bike all the time. I'm glad on both counts. I've always liked that kid."

Janell added, "The few times I saw him he seemed to me to be a pretty typical teenager. Resentful of authority and trying his best to go out on his own. Time will tell if he can pull himself together. I hope his does. Have you talked with your sister lately about what going on with Norman?"

Matt furrowed his brow. "Thank you for reminding me. I should do that. I know at first Lydia was going crazy not knowing where he was or what he was doing. But I am sure that was part of his escape his plan. He did make phone contact with her a couple of times, but he kept her in the dark about where he was. For her as his mother, just knowing he was okay was everything. She actually seemed a little pleased at his progress – sketchy as he kept it. He's not a dummy and so I have confidence eventually he'll do just fine."

****

Unlike Boston, this time Matt bypassed the Schwinn dealer and went by himself to the local Trek store. After looking at a big selection of mountain bikes and road bikes and everything in between, he went away, happily, with an aluminum Trek 520 bicycle. It was much lighter and seemed more agile than Traveler. After he paid for it, he had to fill out a detailed bike registration form and pay $10 for a decal. "This helps the cops with stolen bikes and there are lots of those around here," the salesperson explained.

****

Laredo for the Ramparts crew was an easier set-up than any of their other concert cities. Because of the stifling heat, Rudy had booked Amy's concert into Laredo's air-conditioned First Bank Concert Hall. But Norman and his fellow workers still had a lot of work to do. Amy had agreed to do a song-writing workshop for students at Laredo Community College's music program, which required some stage set-up for her instruments and visuals and seating. Before the concerts she was to receive the Golden Note Award from the Texas Country Music Academy at a big gala where the crew was responsible for the some elaborate staging with backlit video and a complicated sound system. And because the First Bank hall only seated 2,400 there would be two concerts. They weren't back-to-back because of a booking in between which meant they had to do two set-ups and two take-downs. It didn't bother Norman. He thrived on all the activity.

Norman was happy that Laredo was compact enough that he could get anywhere he needed to be – or wanted to be – on Traveler. It did occur to him one day when he stopped at Cassida Laredo for lunch, a famed Tex-Mex restaurant, that maybe he needed a lock for his bike. Cassida was a big and a busy place so he simply leaned it against the building and sat where he could keep an eye on it. But he got a bit anxious when, as he was nearly finished with his chile rellenos, he noticed three teenagers in black clothing sporting red bandanas around their heads carefully inspecting Traveler. He watched them as they seemed to go over it in detail. Should he leave then and make sure his bike wouldn't be stolen? He still had more food, but he got up hurriedly, paid his tab and went outside. They were still going over his bike when he – with a bit of nervousness – approached. They seemed bigger when he got near them outside.

"This your bike?" Norman nodded. "You wanna sell it?"

"No." At which point they thankfully left without saying another word.

At the Schwinn store, Norman bought the strongest cable lock they had. He thought he might do some night riding so they showed him a tiny strobe light that fit under his handlebars. He was told installing the light underneath meant less chance of it being stolen. At the counter he asked the salesperson how to get to the Gateway Bridge. "You thinking about riding across to Mexico?"

"Can I?"

"You'll need a government issued ID. But sure. A bike is the best way to get across, as you'll see. The cars and trucks are usually stacked up so deep it can take several hours to get across. But with a bike you can ride along the walkway and when you get to the checkpoint the Mexican border guards are pretty friendly. Coming back, though, the U.S. guards are really strict. Not nearly as many cars – it's mostly trucks – coming this way, but clearing the border may take twice as long because they're always on the lookout for drugs. The big flow – really the only flow for drugs is this way. The best time to go is early morning or later in the day because of the heat. I wouldn't go across at night. Sure you have a light, but in the dark over there you're more likely to run into trouble. In town riding at night is fine though."

"Thanks for the advice. What's there to see on the other side?"

"If you're thinking of a nice touristy kind of ride in Mexico, forget it. Nuevo Laredo is pretty harsh because it's all big plants and giant warehouses with cheap labor churning out stuff to send back to the US. Nobody from here goes over there unless they have business. And then they come right back. Not to scare you, but now and then there are nasty drug fights over there. Every time that happens there seem to be ugly killings. I don't mean to paint a totally bad picture because it seems to be getting better, or at least we're told that. There are actually four bridges from here to there, but on a bike or as a pedestrian you can only cross on two of them – the Gateway and the Columbia-Solidarity. I read just the other day where Laredo is the largest inland port on the border. Supposedly, according to the article, almost half the U.S. trade with Mexico passes over those four bridges. If you go, I'd ride for a bit over there and then turn around and come back. That way, you can say you've been to Mexico."

After he left the store, of course, riding across the bridge with the possibility of danger on the other side was the pull for Norman. That would make it more fun. He had to ride over the Gateway Bridge if for no other reason to say he had. So he pointed Traveler's front wheel toward the Rio Grande River – and who knew – maybe some adventure.

Before he got on it, Norman stopped to take in the grandeur of the Gateway Bridge. It seemed like a huge span because at this point the Rio Grande was almost half a mile wide and with the entrances at either end it was much longer than that. In the morning light it looked even more majestic. Of course he had to sketch it. He put off his adventure to Mexico for about half an hour as he sketched in the basic shape of the bridge. He could finish it later when he got back to his hotel.

As he made his way across the bridge it was especially fun sailing past about a hundred cars and trucks stuck waiting. As he approached the Mexican checkpoint Norman was surprised to see that there were about a dozen other bikes of all descriptions waiting to be processed, but they and he were through in no time.

Just as soon as he was on the other side, his first impression was how lousy the streets were. Sometimes there were monstrous potholes and frequently no paving whatsoever. He couldn't ride on the sidewalks. They seemed a joke because – he guessed – each building built their own since they didn't match up. It seemed crazy. He chuckled because randomly some sections were wide, others narrow. And others times there was no pedestrian pavement, just like the streets. He wandered for just a bit taking the advice of the bike store guy. But after a few choppy blocks, he felt hungry as he approached a big food truck open on the side. It was the aroma that got him. He leaned Traveler against the truck without locking it.

Norman couldn't read the Spanish menu, but he pointed to tacos and they served him a heaping portion, which he took over to a rickety chair to sit and eat. Like before, as he ate, what looked like a couple of shady characters ambled up and stood beside Traveler. Norman couldn't understand their Spanish but it was apparent they were inspecting his bike. What was the attraction he wondered? It was a Schwinn. Nothing special he could tell. It was bright red, but so were lots of other bikes. Soon they wandered off looking back over their shoulders babbling in Spanish – he assumed – about the bike.

He made it back across the bridge without incident. The Ramparts crew was staying at the Marriott in Laredo, so when he got back Norman went to the front entrance where the bellman said, "You a guest here? Be sure to really lock that thing carefully. It looks like a good bike. They really like ones like that. Best to put it in our garage where it should be safe."

Norman started to ask the bellman, "Everyone seems so concerned about my bike. Why is that?" He barely got out his question when at that very moment a huge, black limo pulled up and signaled for the bellman who bowed deeply as he opened the door for several dark-suited men. So Norman did not get an answer, here at least. He did wonder if the big car and dark suits meant a group of drug dealers had just arrived. But he scolded himself for concentrating too much on the drug scene. But maybe that was because it had some fascination for him and it seemed to pop up in a lot of conversations.

****

There was a message on his hotel phone when he got to his room. It was Rudy calling a crew meeting for that evening.

At the meeting Rudy began, "So this is our last concert in this tour. I think it has been fantastic so far. The opener in Richmond was stunning. The Columbus concert was great, even with the big problem, but that's behind us now. Tallahassee showed our community giving. Wasn't that amazing – all those thousands of kids? What I really liked about Algiers was our ability to adapt to the local scene. I'll never forget Amy in that huge balloon float. At one point it looked like the whole thing might just drift up into the sky. So now we have two performances here in Laredo. I feel bad that we have to set up twice, but that happened because their concert hall is so well booked that the Friday date was the only one I could get that weekend. Saturday was already filled for a play of some kind. But then our first concert sold out so fast I decided to see if we could get another date, which turned out to be Sunday. It's inconvenient I know, but it shows the power of Amy and you wonderful people in putting on top-notch shows. Thank you.

"And as a way to really thank you I have an offer. You will get your regular cash bonuses for all your hard work. But to wrap up this tour and to truly express my appreciation I will take any of you who want to go for a four-day trip to Mexico City – all expenses paid. We're so close, why not? How does that sound?"

After the excited conversation died down, Rudy continued. "I want to express my special thanks to Amy. You are our star – and your fans' star – in so many ways. Please stand and we'll bow to you this time." Besides the unified bow, there was sustained applause from the 30 crew members.

Amy smiled and took it all in. She responded, "I also want to say thank you for the great work of your crew members. All of you – Rudy and Gus and Helen and Naomi and Richard and Jimmy and Norman. I don't mean to leave anyone out. You all are great." And she bowed.

Rudy ended the session by saying, "The last thing I want to mention is to please sign up for the Mexico City tour on your way out. It's planned we will fly down there Monday after our Sunday concert. Those of you who choose not to go, you can hang out here in Laredo until we all get back or you can head back to Richmond on Monday. Oh and one last thing, I promise. It's getting late. Don't forget we have the Golden Note Awards dinner and gala day after tomorrow.

"All of you who want to attend are welcome, but once again, please sign up before you go so we have a head count."

On the way out Norman and Naomi were walking together. She asked, "That Mexico City thing sounds great, so are you going?"

Norman hesitated. "Mexico doesn't impress me. I know it's a neat offer from Rudy, but I may just hang out here. I have to decide."

****

In the main ballroom of the Marriott, the Golden Note Awards ceremony was a glittery show in itself. Many of the legends of country music were at the head table surrounding Amy and as they were introduced one-by-one, a huge portrait appeared on the screen and a piece of their music played in the room. But the highlight of the ceremony was a video of Amy's life introduced by a somewhat disheveled old man. As the video started with her childhood in Hilltop, Tennessee where she was born, the man introduced himself.

He intoned in a twangy accent, "My name is 'Radio Man.' Some of you may have heard me over the years on station KHILL – a true country music station. I am kin to this girl. I knew from the beginning she had big talent, so over the years I took pictures of her and made some recordings. For this video, I dug out a bunch of old photos and put them together with the sound tracks I had. I hope you enjoy it."

First there was an image of six-year-old Amy, her hair in braids in a simple kid's dress, just standing in front of her family's house. Then after several minutes she began singing a soulful tune about the hill country. Her voice was strong for such a young person. The sound was scratchy and missing entirely at one point but her voice was clear and strong – plaintive at times – even at that early age. Her young face turned up at the end of the song almost beseeching the viewer to understand her plight. It was quite emotional.

The applause was muted at first and then grew louder and louder. That one bit of film helped those at the dinner better understand how Amy could – continually and emotionally – stir up her audiences, even as an adult.

The piece covered other stages of her life – from cheerleading in high school, singing in her church and more – and there were repeated whoops and hollers from the audience for the pictures and accompanying music. At one point Norman looked around and noticed there were six television cameras recording the whole thing. He leaned over to Naomi and said, "Look at all those cameras. This really is a bigger deal than I thought."

In a low voice she asked, "What are you doing after this?"

"I don't know. Nothing planned."

"I've had several glasses of wine at dinner, but do you want to have a something to drink after this?"

When they were settled in a far dark corner of the hotel bar Naomi asked, "Have you decided about going with the gang to Mexico City yet?"

Norman considered his answer. "I know this may not be fair to a whole country, but a couple of days ago I rode my bike over one of the bridges into Mexico. The riding was fun but I really didn't like it over there. From the little I saw, it's nothing like what we're used to. At one point I wasn't sure if my bike might be ripped off. Was I scared? I guess. There were these two thugs looking over my Traveler bike while I ate a taco."

"Sounds like they probably would've had your lunch, if they wanted. You really like that bike don't you?" She got a little closer. "But what else didn't you like about Mexico?"

"As I said when I stopped for a bite to eat, a couple of – what to me looked like bad guys – appeared and were going over my bike almost like they wanted to steal it right in front of me. I was right there so they didn't, but it bothered me that I had no idea what they were saying or what they maybe wanted to do. So I think I'll pass on Rudy's offer."

Naomi paused for a moment after she ordered another glass of wine.

"Do you remember Danny from the party I had in Amy's bus in Tallahassee? Well I can hardly get away from him. After Rudy announced the trip to Mexico he came up to me and said, 'This is great. Why don't we hook up down there? Perfect place to do it.' But I don't want anything to do with him. He's a creep."

"So does this mean you won't be going either?"

"Can I be honest? I'd rather stay here and we can hang out together. We're friends. I know this is ballsy on my part but I'd rather shack up with you. How about that?"

Maybe Norman should have seen something like this coming from Naomi. He didn't think he had invited it in any way. Hoped he hadn't. He shook his head and said emphatically, "Forget that. I like you as a friend, but you met Ricky in New Orleans. I've never met anyone like her. She means everything to me."

Before the group left for Mexico, Norman found out Naomi was a one of the passengers. As far as he knew he was the only one to stay back.

****

After everyone got back from the bonus trip to Mexico, Norman planned on driving back in the equipment truck with Gus. But while they were gone Norman had four days to relax and explore more of Laredo. He considered another trip this time across the Columbia-Solidarity Bridge, but it didn't excite him.

He got on Traveler in the cooler mornings and late afternoons to explore the town. Where he spent a good deal of time was in Old Town Laredo, probably because it reminded him in some ways of the old section of Richmond. During the hottest part of the day he enjoyed a shaded chaise lounge between swims in the Marriott pool. Thoughts of Ricky were always in the front of his mind, so on the second day he got up and went to his room to call her.

Just as he started to dial her in Richmond, he sat back on the bed when another thought crowded into his head. He could hardly wait to talk with Ricky, but before that maybe he should call his mother. He couldn't remember exactly how long but he thought it had been several weeks since he reported his whereabouts to Lydia. He hesitated and then dialed her in Alexandria. As the phone rang, he tried to make a quick decision about whether to tell his mother about Ricky.

After eight rings the voice recording came on. He was stunned when a male voice said, "Cheerio. You have reached Brian and Lydia. We're not here right now, but after the beep, please leave a message and we'll get back to you right away." Norman hung up immediately. Brian and Lydia. What was that all about? The voice sounded funny. Some sort of foreign accent. Was this the same guy he saw on that morning in his mother's kitchen? He'd had no warning, so Norman wasn't sure what to make of this development with his mother. Should he be mad? Should he be glad? He sat for what seemed like a long time on the bed with all kinds of thoughts going through his head. He wished Ricky were here to help him sort it out.

But then, slowly, it came to him. He had his life now. He liked his life now. Why shouldn't she have her life? It amazed him that he might like her life with Brian. As he thought about this situation he realized over the past couple of years he had given her enough trouble. It was clear to him that that was in the past and would stop. Brian was still a question mark for Norman, but maybe he was a good guy. Norman dialed the Alexandria number again and after the beep left this message. "Hi. This is Norman. Sorry I haven't called more often, but we've been very busy. Our concerts are finished now so I will have more time. I am in Texas at the moment planning to go back to my job in Richmond in a few days. Things are really good for me. I've met a wonderful woman. I will call more often." How should he end this? "I hope things are good for you too – both of you. Love you mom."

At first he was glad he could leave the message he did on voicemail because it made it much easier than speaking with her. She always had a lot of questions. But in his gut he knew he would rather have spoken with his mother in person.

****

He did reach Ricky later. He told her about his brief trip to Mexico; about the awards ceremony and the concerts; how he decided not to go to Mexico again with the crew; how when they got back he and Gus would drive back to Richmond in their truck; how he missed her intensely and could hardly wait a week to see her.

She got him going when she said, "Wasn't Algiers fun? I'll never forget it. Especially the way you treated me in the

Secret Garden. I've never experienced anything like that before. You are a great lover. I know I've told you that before, but I needed to say it again. I'll just have to come up with a Secret Garden up here. Wouldn't that be fun? But we don't have magnolia trees in Virginia. At least I don't think we do. But I know some other ways to excite you."

Norman was pleased with what she just said – pleased that Ricky would say things like that to him on the phone. He was glad she couldn't see him, though, because her words made him self-conscious. And as usual there was a swelling in his trousers.

To change the subject he asked how the boat repairs were coming along.

"We should be back in the water in a few weeks. Besides the repairs from the fire, I decided to also do some of the changes we meant to make some time ago."

He asked, "Like what? The Belle seems perfect to me."

"For one thing we're changing out all the seats. We're had some comments that the old ones are uncomfortable and I think they are old looking. Eric doesn't agree, but I'm changing the hull color from the light blue to a dark green. More like the original.

"Matter of fact, Eric and I have had several arguments over Belle since she was hauled out. I'm not sure what's going on with him. He doesn't show up when he says he will. And he seems surly at times when we do meet. This is just a thought, but I remember way back when he was headed for college he wanted to study art, but our father forced him to get an engineering degree. Maybe he wants out. Maybe he wants to be an artist full time. Our father left us enough money so he could do that and not worry about making a living. I just don't know."

Norman decided it was best to stay out of that family discussion.

****

The next day Norman partook of one of Laredo's top tourist activities. He went down to a dock by the Rio Grande and signed up for a two-hour river-rafting trip. "Plan to get wet," the guide said and they did, mostly by splashing the river water on themselves. It was refreshing in the heat and none of his fellow passengers had any complaints. Their guide made a point of sticking to the U.S. side.

"This river marks the boundary between the two countries, and because we're a U.S. outfit, we could get arrested for wandering onto the Mexico side. So we're very careful about that. We don't want to give any impression we're involved with drugs. Matter of fact we meet with the Mexican border patrol people all the time to make sure they see us as only – and I emphasize only – a U.S. tourist attraction."

After the bus came back from downriver and delivered him to the hotel, he asked the bellman about a good Italian restaurant he had heard about somewhere in west Laredo. "You must mean Café Sistina. Northern Italian. Very good. Lots of food. Authentic." And he gave Norman directions.

When he got to the restaurant on Traveler, he realized he hadn't brought his new lock. What to do? He couldn't exactly take his bike inside with him. And the small windows meant he couldn't sit and watch the bike as he had done several times before. Around the corner he spotted a valet parking attendant and went over to see if he could help.

"I forgot my lock. Any chance I can leave my bike with you?"

"You can but I move around a lot. I'll try my best, but no guarantees. Put it over by the back door. Nice bike." And with that he hurriedly left to park a car for a restaurant patron. Norman was anxious but what could he do? He was unsure whether to tip the attendant now or later. He decided later.

He was hungry so he splurged on the food. He started with Caprese. Fresh Mozzarella, tomato, and basil dressed with balsamic vinaigrette. Next was Insalata Contadina. Mixed greens with arugula, cremini mushrooms, bell peppers, sweet onions with a mango vinaigrette. For a main course he decided on Salsiccia al Chianti. Italian sausages sautéed with onions and garlic in a spicy tomato sauce with penne. It was quite a meal.

Norman had paid his bill and was headed out the front door to the parking lot when he heard a commotion from around the corner. Someone was yelling profanities. "You fucking Mexicans. I'll call the cops. You bastards." He heard running and just as he got to where he had left Traveler, he saw the parking attendant wrestling with three guys in dark clothing. They had grabbed Traveler with the attendant trying to keep them from tossing it into the back of a van. Norman rushed over, but it was too late. The two of them were no match for what seemed like massive thieves. As the van peeled out of the parking area, Norman squinted to get the license number. But it was covered up.

"I'm sorry, man. I had my back turned for a few seconds and those assholes snuck behind me and grabbed your bike. Now I wish I hadn't agreed to watch your bike. I can call the cops for you."

The police arrived within a few minutes. Norman described the vehicle as best he could as what looked like a white 1980 Chevy van. No special markings and no license number though. He didn't have a description of the thieves except to say there were three of them and they were about all about six feet tall. The attendant couldn't add anything more. Norman asked, "Why would they want to steal my bike? It's nothing special. Just a pretty ordinary Schwinn."

The policeman replied, "If only we knew the criminal mind better. I hate to say it but a stolen bike is nothing compared to most of the stuff we deal with every day. Here's our report for your insurance claim. We sometimes recover stolen bikes, but when we do they are usually trashed. Oh, by the way. Do you have a license for this bike?"

"Actually I'm just visiting. From Virginia. Do you know about the Amy Concerts? I was working with them. Going back in a few days."

****

Norman felt lost without Traveler. Later in the afternoon he went back to the Schwinn store where he bought the lock. He wanted to see if they would rent him a bike for a couple of days. Randy the sales person wanted to know and he asked what happened.

After Norman related the details of the theft, Randy asked, "Where did you get the bike in the first place? Ah, it's from Boston originally and I'll bet they don't register them there, right? Then I'm pretty sure I know what happened. Bikes in Laredo – and all of Texas for that matter – have to be registered. That means they can be traced easily. Lately I've heard through the bike grapevine that the lowlifes have been searching for bikes without registrations and we think it's because they can ride them across the border without being traced. Are they using them to transport drugs? Who knows? I'm sure you've heard some of the crazy ways drugs are coming across the river and elsewhere over the border. But here the international traffic is so busy the border patrol people go nuts trying to figure out every scheme. It's become a giant game and guess who's winning?"

Now it made sense to Norman why groups had stopped periodically to examine Traveler.

****

Once across the border the white Chevy van hurried to a warehouse deep in Nuevo Laredo. Inside, the Traveler was pulled out and taken over to a dark corner. A mechanic took a wrench and loosened the seat post and pulled it and the seat out in one swift move. A tallish young girl held slender plastic bags of white powder that she very carefully stuffed all the way down the seat tube until there was just enough space left so the seat post could be re-installed. It went back in in seconds. Traveler looked exactly as it had when it came in moments ago. The last step was to have one of their drug sniffing dogs go over Traveler and test it for any traces of drugs, just as the border guards would do. Sniff. Sniff. Sniff. Nothing because of the steel of the bike frame. They opened a side door and she was off on Traveler all within ten minutes, pedaling at a leisurely pace, headed for the U.S. border.

****

The day before the troops were to come back from Mexico City, Norman was wandering around the old section of Laredo whose entrance was a wide five-way intersection. On Babcock Street he stopped in one shop after another. A corner bookshop caught his interest and so he went in. "Any books on bikes?" The clerk disappeared and came back with three. He browsed through them and decided to buy the one they had on bike touring in New England. If he didn't like it, he could give it to Uncle Matt.

As he went out onto the sidewalk the pedestrian light at the intersection turned green and so he stepped into the wide crosswalk. As he glanced to his left he could see several cars that were lined up behind the red light some distance from him because of the five-way intersection. On the left side of the line of stopped cars was a red bike that caught his eye. He stopped, looked carefully and fleetingly thought it looked like Traveler with a girl riding it. But it couldn't be. Or could it? The thieves who took Traveler had been men, so he took another couple of steps. But he sensed something was wrong when he looked again and noticed the same exact under-handlebar light they had sold him when he bought his lock. It was very noticeable to him.

Now the cars and the bike were coming toward him and as he quickly glanced down, he knew it had to Traveler when he spotted the obvious BBB sticker on the seat tube. It came very close and nearly knocked him over. He first yelled, "Hey. That's my bike. Get off it." She paid no attention and so he reacted by trying to grab his bike. Traffic was getting snarled at this point. She kicked at him to get him away and a sort of wrestling match started between them. Norman had a moment of hesitation to get in a fight with a girl, but when she kicked him in the groin, he got very mad and decided to get back his bike, no matter what.

This had turned serious. Several people had come up to see what was going on and the tussle with the two of them became nasty as she grabbed at his hair and he pulled at her clothes with the bike between them. Norman kept yelling, "Get off my bike. Give me my bike." Their fight was halted in a flash when a volley of shots rang out from a passing car. Norman dropped the bike as she ran trying to reach the disappearing car. Then he felt a deep stinging in his leg and reached down to feel a gush of blood. It made him topple over in pain.

Doubled over as he was, he thought he saw the people who fired the gun try to grab the bike and quickly stuff it in their car, but it was too big so they tossed it aside. The girl sprinted away and just made it into the disappearing car. They took off just as the wail of a police siren got close. So there was Norman, writhing in pain beside Traveler as the cops appeared.

****

The ambulance ran him to the South Texas Medical Center Emergency Room in what seemed like a few seconds. He felt delirious so he wasn't sure of the timing – or at that point of anything else. He was told he actually had two gunshot wounds in the leg, but the EMTs had stopped the bleeding, so it was about ten minutes before he was wheeled into the actual ER and lifted from the gurney onto the operating table. He hurt. Everything was a blur and it didn't help that the overheard lights were so bright Norman had to close his eyes completely. The only time he got close to an ER before was in Columbus after the skydiving crisis when he wasn't a patient. Soon he could hear voices telling the doctor sketchy details of what had happened. Apparently his ears were just fine because he clearly heard the blurry white coat to his left say, "I can't believe it. This is my nephew. Norman, how did you get here?" He opened his eyes and fuzzily saw his Uncle Matt. How could this happen? How could he have been shot? How could he and a familiar face be in the same ER? Norman wanted to get up – at least sit up – and embrace him but now the pain was so strong he closed his eyes again and practically passed out.

The nurse looked confused – puzzled – as Matt said, "Let's get you fixed up first. Then tomorrow maybe we can figure this whole thing out. Let me see that leg. The EMT told me you have two wounds in your right leg."

****

On his rounds the next day, Matt headed straight for Norman's room. "It's hard for me to believe you are in this town in this hospital – and I am your attending physician. We can talk about this coincidence and about what happened a bit later, but for right now I don't know if you know it, but you are a lucky guy. Since I first saw you, the police told me the bad guys fired about ten bullets to keep you away from your bike. But you got two serious hits. It was our Traveler, wasn't it? I'm amazed. Your wounds should heal just fine, but we want to keep you in the hospital for a couple of days for observation."

Norman couldn't really believe any of it either.

Matt continued. "When I told Janell what happened, she was amazed too. She insisted you come to our house after we get you out of here. You'll be on crutches for a while but other than that you should be mobile. Oh, by the way, have you told your mother where you are?"

Before Norman responded, he was reminded he hadn't called Ricky either. "I just called my mother a couple of days ago. Had to leave a message. For me – at first – it was a surprise when Brian's voice was on the voice recording. I think I feel pretty good about them, but do you know what that's all about?"

Matt was examining Norman's wounds as he said, "These look like you are healing very well. There was some bone damage, but while you were still under the anesthesia in the ER, I brought in an excellent orthopedic doc and he feels you won't be hampered in any way. You'll have scars, but heck, I do too. Now about Brian and my sister. It's all good stuff, but I have to get to the rest of my rounds so why don't we talk about them when you get to our house? Actually, Janell knows more about them than I do. She is planning to pick you up at three this afternoon when you are discharged from the hospital." Matt sat on the edge of Norman's bed – not as a doctor would normally do but because they were relatives and friends. "This probably is not the best way for us to get together but who would have ever believed we would end up in the same town in the same hospital? I think it's great we met up no matter how it happened. See you at our house."

Before Matt left, Norman told him, "It's hard to believe and I don't know if you know it, but we've been in an ER together before."

"That's impossible. Why didn't I know that? Why didn't you tell me?"

"I will. At your house."

Around midday two men in suits knocked on Norman's door. He had been dozing, so he sat up quickly when they introduced themselves as detectives from the Laredo Police Crime Unit. They asked how he was feeling. "Fine. Fine. Turns out my doctor is my uncle. Just by coincidence."

"Good. That's interesting. He says you're recovering well. Do you feel up to talking with us about what happened yesterday?" Norman nodded. He was never comfortable around police officers of any kind. "We know your bicycle was stolen from Café Sistina Restaurant three days before and neither you or the parking attendant could give any description of the perpetrators or the vehicle except they were in a white van. Is that correct so far?""

Norman nodded again and said, "Why would they steal such an ordinary bike like mine?"

"We've learned you actually have a very valuable bicycle to drug runners for several reasons. They can't buy a bicycle anywhere in Texas without it being registered and that means any of those bikes can be traced. They can try to take off the decal the bike dealer must put on, but it's almost impossible and when they do it always leaves clear marks. Turns out that's happened a couple of times recently at the border and the guards have orders to confiscate those bicycles until the rider can prove they own it. But because you are a visitor with a bike from another state – with no decal because your state must not require them like Texas – no problem."

"That's interesting because a couple of times I noticed my bike being carefully inspected by groups I assume were drug runners."

"Stashing drugs in bicycle tubes is a new one for us. More creativity. More for us to do. Because we were able to recover your bike, it might interest you to know it held $40,000 worth of cocaine – in that one tube. The street value of what we recovered is probably three times that amount."

Norman said, "I see. They must have taken out the seat post, stuffed the drugs down the seat tube and put the seat back like nothing was different. Pretty clever. It would be too difficult to do the same thing with the other bike tubes as you probably figured out. It's hard to believe, though, that my Traveler bike was hauling that much money around."

The taller police officer responded, "Because it was worth so much, we believe they had a series of cars that would act as outriders to accompany the bike and protect its valuable stash. We also believe the shots that struck you were from one of those cars. But you were very, very lucky because we recovered ten bullets from the scene. Either they were poor shots or they decided not to kill you."

"I'm happy about that. Thank goodness." Norman shook his head and waited for a few moments before asking, "I know this may seem like a small matter, but where's my bike now?"

"We have it in our property room at the police station. We need to hang on to it for evidence. It may be some time until we find the perps and take them to trial. After that happens we'll notify you and we can ship it back to you. Anything else you want to add or questions you have?"

After they left Norman picked up the phone and called Ricky in Richmond. He told her everything. She was shocked. And then mad before she grasped the whole thing. She was amazed too at the coincidence with Uncle Matt. "That makes me feel good, though, because I know you are getting the best care possible. I love you. Come back as soon as you can."

"I will. I love you too."

The Wedding

On the way to their house Janell asked if there was anything special Norman would like to eat or read or do. "I take it your silence means you're okay. We're so happy to have you stay with us. Matt has filled me in on some of the details. It sounds horrible. And he says you are very lucky."

"The cops said that too," Norman responded.

"I don't know if I should tell you this but Matt treating you in the hospital is not the usual. Normally doctors don't treat their relatives, but Matt told me he insisted he take care of you. That's because he thinks a lot of you."

"Thanks. I appreciate Uncle Matt, too. Honestly, I was really surprised – but really glad to see him in the ER... although I didn't recognize him at first because of the fog I was in. After the shooting, I think seeing him there made me want to heal quicker."

****

Over Texas barbeque in Matt and Janell's backyard, the three of them talked a lot about their various adventures. Norman told them about leaving Alexandria on his mother's bike, the one Matt sold her in Boston. Their beloved Traveler.

"My life has changed a lot since then. I think the bike is about the only thing that hasn't changed for me – except as you know, the police are holding it for evidence."

"We'll get it back eventually. Where were your other concerts?" Matt asked.

It was easy for Norman to tell them about his job – what was fun, what was difficult, and which places they played for concerts. What was a little harder – and he didn't know why – was telling them about Ricky. At first he was reluctant to tell them about her probably because of their age difference, but once he got started it all poured out. How he met her. Her river boat. Their time together in Algiers. His passion for her.

Janell spoke first. "It sounds like love to me."

"This is all so new for me," Norman said. "On my own with nobody to tell me what to do. A job I really like where I can support myself. And a woman. Ricky means everything to me. It is love."

Matt told of first going to Lackland and then being sent here to Laredo. "Because I think the general at the hospital there, for all his apparent toughness, was really a coward at heart. But who knows? If that hadn't happened perhaps we wouldn't have connected again. Janell and I think he did us a big favor."

Matt continued. "Norman you mentioned when I treated you here that we had been together in the ER – it seems way back – in Columbus. I couldn't tell if that was because you were delirious from the sedatives I gave you after the shooting. I surely would have known if you were there – even though it was mayhem with all those people to be treated. That seems nearly impossible. What was that all about?"

"I definitely wasn't a patient in the ER. But we were probably no more than 50 feet apart on several occasions.

Neither of us knew it then. You remember the accident with the skydivers in Columbus? I'll never forget that. I was assigned to an ambulance that went back and forth from the accident to the ER. I usually didn't go directly into the ER. Just helped the EMTs move people. The few times I saw inside, it was docs in masks and gowns and head coverings – all of them working so hard. There's no way I would have known you were at the hospital at Fort Benning during our hospital runs. It was so busy. I only learned it the next day when our boss got the team together and went over the events of the night before."

Matt and Janell could barely believe the coincidence.

"Among the things my boss told us about was that he had spoken with one of the ER docs who treated the injured people that night, a Dr. Hudson, who said the television cameraman – the one with the broken neck who they rushed by helicopter to Atlanta – was doing fine and would probably make a full recovery. When I heard that my first question was – What? Could the Dr. Hudson he talked about be my uncle? Of all places. Why would he be in Columbus? I got pretty excited. But it was a big meeting with the brass from Fort Benning. It would have been embarrassing to leave then. I wasn't sure what to do. How to find you – if it was you? Soon as I could I borrowed a car. I was worried about speeding over to the main gate at Fort Benning."

"What happened?"

"The huge armed guard at the gate wouldn't let me in. No military ID, no sticker on the car, so there was no way he would let me in there. I pleaded with him to call the hospital. At least he did that. He tried but they wouldn't give out any information. They wouldn't leave Dr. Hudson a message even. So there I was. I didn't know what to do. And we were leaving the next morning early. I felt terrible, but what could I do?"

"It was nice of you to try," Janell said. "But we're together now. Another coincidence, but a good one, except for your accident.

Matt didn't go into any detail, but he did relate some of what now seemed like the terrible nonsense he went through in Boulder. "So we've both been through our traumas. And we're both okay. That's what counts. Wonderful to have you with us, Norman."

Norman had a question. "As I mentioned to Matt in the hospital when I called my mother, the voice recording was Brian's voice. When I called her back later, it was to tell her about my accident and about us being together in Laredo. She was pretty upset, but thankful I'm OK, and thankful and surprised about you being here too. We didn't get a chance to talk about the Brian thing at the time, but what's up with that?"

Janell took that one. "It's very exciting. But maybe you don't know. And maybe it shouldn't come from us, but Brian and your mother are getting married. In about three weeks."

Everyone looked at each other and no one spoke just then. The impending marriage all of a sudden seemed like a touchy subject.

After several moments Matt said, "I know this news should have come from Lydia, but now that it's out you will be going to the wedding, won't you? I know your mother will want you there. I have an idea. Janell, why don't we leave Norman alone so he can call her?" Norman did, and he told her all about Ricky.

****

Ricky met Norman in front of Ramparts after Gus dropped him off. She had him in a tight embrace and wouldn't let him talk for several minutes. "I see the crutches. But you get around pretty well. I'm so happy to have you back here. It's not time now but when we get to my house – I really want you to live with me and not on the boat – I have some news for you."

"And I have some for you."

****

They were snuggled on the couch in her living room as much as they could with his leg sticking straight out because of his cast. He asked, "So what's your news?"

"You remember that time I spoke with you on the phone when you were in Laredo about how strange I thought Eric was acting with the boat out of the water? Well it got worse. He seemed belligerent most of the time. Uncooperative. Well I was right. He wants to pursue his art and he doesn't want anything to do with Belle any more. He wants me to buy him out, which I'm more than willing to do especially with his attitude lately. We haven't settled on a price, but I don't think there will be a problem."

"Is that good news for you?"

"In more ways than one. I'm perfectly happy doing the whole business myself, which I was practically doing anyway. The other thing that makes me happy about Eric getting out is – and I have to be careful about how I say this – I'd like you to consider eventually being my new partner. You don't have to say anything now. And if you decide to stay with Ramparts, I am perfectly fine with that too. I've thought a lot about whether being in business together and being lovers – whether that might screw up our relationship. Please understand I do not want anything to come between us. I figure if we both go in with that assumption, if the business thing doesn't work out and you go do something else, we still have each other. That's more important to me than anything."

Norman had a lot to think about. He said, "That is some news. I remember a couple of things you said. Thinking back you probably had some idea that might happen. Nothing will come between us. Let me think about it. I love you."

He kissed Ricky a long time. In the midst of their passionate kiss, he wondered how they would make love with his heavy cast, but he knew they would figure it out. When they were finished nuzzling and kissing he said, "Okay. Now for my news. I was really surprised – amazed – that in a phone conversation with my mother a couple of days ago, she told me she is getting married to her boyfriend Brian. He's an Australian my mother met while she was riding Traveler to work back in D.C."

Ricky said, "That bike has a way of working itself into a lot of our situations. So this was big news for you?"

"Yes. Actually, Brian was the reason I took off in the first place. Truthfully, though, maybe his embracing my mother in the kitchen one morning –ahem – nude and with a stiffy – was just an excuse for me to run. I've thought a lot about my mother and Brian and in fact I'm pretty happy for her. Uncle Matt asked why I should judge Brian before I got to know him. And he's right. So here's the best part. She really wants me to come to the wedding in a couple of weeks. That gave me a reason to tell her all about you. I told her I would only come if you go too. Her response was 'I love you enormously Norman. I insist you bring Ricky.'"

****

The ceremony and reception were set up on the lawn at the Potomac Yacht Club. Beautiful day. Clear blue skies. The view of the District across the Potomac was like a giant mural. Everything was picture perfect for their wedding. The bar was open so as soon as the guests arrived they could have a drink. The food was also laid out in the club's big tent. Some guests nibbled as they waited for the event to get underway at four o'clock.

At 3:45 in the afternoon, Lydia broke into a conversation Brian was having with three of her colleagues. "Can I borrow this wonderful man for a few moments?" She took him aside and with a frown said, "We're about to start and I don't see your best man. And almost none of your guests are here. Do you know what is going on?"

"Nigel is notoriously late. He'll be along. The guests seem happy. Give them a drink and some food and they'll be fine. Okay?" And he gave her a big smooch.

Nobody really noticed the time except Lydia. When she suddenly looked at her watch again, it said 4:25 and she became more worried. She scouted out Brian again and found him in the rear part of the tent sitting with three different women. "Hi darling. I need to speak with you." Outside the tent she said, "What is going on? The guests are working through the food to say nothing of the liquor. Have you noticed that the ice sculpture of the Opera House on the food table has nearly melted? It looks like a dying bird. Aren't you worried? Everyone may be drunk by the time we start our vows. What should we do? And I don't see a single one of your guests. I need to ask you again – what should we do?"

"Nothing yet. Let's give it another half hour."

"Half an hour. Surely the booze will be gone to say nothing of the food. Then what?"

Just then they heard a honking noise coming around the point at south end of yacht club. It seemed like no one noticed but Brian and Lydia. What they saw was a 50-foot sailboat loaded with people make its way slowly to the yacht club dock. Everyone on board held drinks or bottles of champagne and they were singing at the top of their lungs the Australian wedding song. Repeated blasts of the boat horn got everyone's attention and the bumpy landing told the story of what they had been doing all this time.

Brian put his arm around Lydia and said, "No. I didn't know a thing about this. But it's very Aussie. Having a wonderful time, though late. Boisterous, wouldn't you say?"

Lydia smiled at last and hugged Brian. "Hell. Let's go down and greet them." She knew by now that Aussies love to have fun no matter what they were doing. With all the commotion the guests were streaming down to the water's edge. The captain, if he really was the captain, announced through a megaphone, "Ladies and gentlemen, please be aware of the arrival of Her Majesty's Ship – the HMS Brilydia – or is it the HMS Lydian? No matter. Let's have a toast." And with that someone unfurled a huge banner from the top of the mast that said, "Congratulations…we think," the latter in small letters.

The crowd on shore raised their glasses and shouted after the captain, "Ahoy. Triple ahoy. Triple ahoy for Lydia and Brian. May they have a wonderful journey – like we've just had." After the toast Lydia nudged Brian. "Now I see where your guests were. But we can't start until you best man arrives. Where could he be?"

Just then the captain called the crowd to attention again. "Ladies and gentlemen, may I present the Honorable Nigel Barnstable, the most worthy Best Man in all the kingdom." And with that the crowd on the boat parted slightly and, with several hands helping steady him, a gentleman in a formal bright blue tuxedo, yellow socks and shiny opera pumps stepped from the boat to the dock followed by a basset hound. The hound raced ahead as Nigel slowly made his way toward Brian and Lydia.

Brian couldn't resist. "I see you brought Sir Oliver with you. Nice to have you both here. Shall we get underway? Come meet the preacher."

The ceremony was traditional simplicity at its best. Except for Brian responding to the preacher, "With this wing – I mean ring" – it all went splendidly. Norman timed it. It took exactly nine minutes for them to be officially married. The traditional kiss took two minutes after which there was much applause when the preacher said, "And now you can make a joyful noise."

****

There was enough food left to make for a gala dinner party before the more formal part of the program began. But Brian had a worry the liquor and wine were getting low so that there might not be enough for the many expected toasts to follow. So during the meal he dispatched Matt and Norman to get more supplies in close-by Alexandria. When they came back they noticed about six people in line behind the captain who was also the emcee. The captain announced that the toasts would be quotes from famous people.

First a man stepped forward and said, "This one is for Brian, an Aussie from the Empire, I mean Commonwealth. Do you know what Prince Phillip said about marriage? He said, 'When a man opens the door for his wife, it's either a new car or a new wife." Subdued laughter, mostly from the men.

The next person was a Brian's roommate before he met Lydia who said, "Zsa Zsa Gabor had it right when she said, 'Why does a woman work ten years to change her husband's habits and then complains that he's not the man she married?'" Big laughter.

A female guest came to the microphone and said in her

best Aussie accent, "At a cocktail party one woman said to her friend, 'Aren't you wearing your wedding ring on the wrong finger?' Her friend replied, 'Yes. I married the wrong man.'" This one was for the female guests who whooped and hollered.

By now the crowd had enough more to drink that the party had become raucous. There was one last toast from a male guest. "Getting married for sex is like buying a 747 for the peanuts." The women showed good arm strength in the fusillade of dinner rolls aimed at his head. Then they booed him off the stage. The men dared not agree. Then the laughter started.

After all was said and done, Lydia stood and said, "I get to have the last word. Here goes. Brian. You are my best friend, my confidant and one of my favorite pests. I say that out of love because you pester me to do things I probably would never do. You make me laugh, you make me cry. You are honest and wise. You are my strength and you are kind-hearted. I will always love you no matter what."

The guests stood and applauded as the bride and groom kissed and hugged.

****

Outside the tent after most of the guests had left Uncle Matt asked Norman, "So are you happy we're all together again?"

Norman said, "Couldn't be happier." He put his arm around Ricky's waist and said, "Especially with Ricky here with me. I can tell the question on your mind and yes, it went very well with Ricky and my mom. She's a tri-athlete now, so all the two of them talked about was their 'PBs' or their Personal Bests in running and biking."

Norman had a sly grin on his face as Ricky used two fingers to reach for a scoop of white frosting from the wedding cake – and placed it on his tongue.

Pau.

Acknowledgements

It goes without saying that one cannot write a book without help. Lots of it. Jay and Jayne Kim own a Schwinn/Raleigh store in Honolulu called Eki Cyclery, which is over 100 years old. They dug around in their archives and were wonderful in supplying photos from catalog pages and general information about the 1980 Schwinn Traveler this book is based on. My skydiving source is a successful businessman named Michel Vinet who is so passionate about his sport that he estimates he has made 5,000 dives since he started around 2000. His caveat about the sky diving in this book was, "This could only happen in the movies." For medical help I turned to Ruth Koehl, who rose to the elite ranks of nursing both in several hospitals and as a national medical device trainer for Johnson & Johnson. My high school buddy Alex Hunter, who was District Attorney in Boulder, Colorado for 28 years, looked over the legal aspects of this story and made excellent suggestions in a complicated chapter toward the end of the book. I know next to nothing about the military so I contacted a good friend Bob Sandla, who among his other career successes rose to Lt. Col. in the Army. He helped with how military rank works and clues on military-speak. Psychology professor (and former clinical sex therapist) Elaine Hatfield at the University of Hawaii was my counselor on the love scenes. A talented art director I have great respect for, Sam Kim, did the cover and inside map. And my editor, Lynn Shizumura, is a gem. Besides her editing skills, she somehow can be gentle and tough at the same time. Thank you all.

Join the fun by adding your comments on this book at:
travelerbike.blogspot.com
Thank you.

Other books by David Cheever

Daytrips Hawaii
Daytrips San Francisco
Pohaku
Belt Collins
A Close Call
Historic Corridors
Envision